WAY BACK WHEN

Nostalgic Essays of
"Growing Up North"

by Jerry Harju

WAY BACK WHEN

Nostalgic Essays of
"Growing Up North"

by Jerry Harju

Cover Design by Stacey Willey
Edited by Pat Green and Karen Murr

Copyright 2004
Jerry Harju

Published by North Harbor Publishing
Marquette, Michigan

Publishing Coordination by
Globe Printing, Inc.
Ishpeming, Michigan

Printed by Sheridan Books, Ann Arbor, Michigan

ISBN 0-9670205-8-1
Library of Congress Control Number 2003113939

April 2004

INTRODUCTION

In the year 2000 I put out a book, "Here's what I think...," a collection of my early newspaper columns published in the *Mining Journal* in Marquette, Michigan. I've pumped out many columns since that book, and again I've selected my favorites. This is a feel-good book, mostly about misadventures of my younger days. I hope you like them.

That's me and my dog, Teddy, on the cover, standing in front of my backyard hideout. You may not believe this, but my pal Jeff and I built that hideout—when we were eight years old! What? You say you *DO* believe it?

Jerry Harju
North Harbor Publishing
528 E. Arch St.
Marquette, MI 49855
Toll Free (877) 906-3984
E-mail: jharju@chartermi.net
Website: www.jerryharju.com

DEDICATION

To Lidia, whose spirit kept me young at heart.

ACKNOWLEDGMENTS

I wish to express my appreciation to the staff of the *Mining Journal* for originally publishing these essays. Special thanks to Dave Edwards, Diane Biery, and Debby Pascoe in the newsroom for giving me specific help when I needed it. I thank my good friends, Jeff Jacobs and Lidia Menchaca for prodding my memory on many of these stories while lunching at Peggy Sue's Cafe. Sadly, Lidia died in a tragic auto accident before this book went to print. The book is dedicated to her memory. My long-suffering editors, Pat Green and Karen Murr, as usual, deserve special acknowledgment for their contributions of bringing class to my prose. As always, kudos to Stacey Willey of Globe Printing for performing an excellent job on the cover design and page layout.

CONTENTS

Books by Jerry Harju

IN THE ALLEYS OF YESTERYEAR

J eff and Lidia and I were having lunch at Peggy Sue's Cafe the other day, and we got to talking about the fact that kids don't play "Cowboys" anymore.

When we were small, Jeff and I were inspired by the double-feature shoot-em-ups at the Ishpeming Theater on Saturday afternoons. We loved movies like *Spoilers of the Range, Two-Gun Town Tamers, Six-Gun Serenade,* and other epic tales featuring Gene Autry, Roy Rogers, Ken Maynard, and Tex Ritter.

In order to be a properly outfitted cowboy back then you had to start with a good toy gun. In 1940 the five-and-dime stores had a wide selection of pistols, but the top-of-the-line was a cap gun. You inserted a roll of caps—a long strip of red paper impregnated with small spots of gunpowder—into the pistol which fed the caps under the hammer as you pulled the trigger, producing a loud "BANG!" This was much better than yelling "POW! POW!" all the time. And just like in the old westerns the cap gun would fire at least twenty shots without reloading. But cap guns were notoriously unreliable, and if you had a good one that worked all the time, you treasured it. In the Gene Autry movies when the bad guys ran out of bullets they would throw the empty guns at Gene. We never did that with a good cap gun. It was much too valuable.

Once you had your gun then you had to learn how to be quick on the draw. One year Jeff's uncle bought him a new gun and holster for his birthday. He told Jeff that in order to become quick on the draw he had to practice in front of a mirror, and when he could outdraw the kid in the mirror then he was really fast. For hours Jeff practiced and practiced in his parents' bedroom but could never beat that kid in the mirror. Although Jeff thought that when he got older he was pretty sure he could have taken him.

Two guns—one on each hip—was the optimum in firepower. With two cap pistols you could blast the one-gunners right out of their socks. However, sometimes the out-gunned kids would start throwing rocks or iron-ore chunks which, of course, evened up the odds quite a bit.

We had most of our gunfights in the Ishpeming alleys because there were plenty of garbage cans to hide behind. As we traded hot lead, we would yell "KA-CHING! KA-CHING!" as our imaginary bullets ricocheted off the metal cans. You couldn't do that these days with garbage cans made of plastic.

We never used broomsticks or anything like that for pretend horses because that would have looked too cutesy. Instead we "galloped" around with a sort of an off-stride polka step, slapping our rumps to make the "horse" go faster, all the while making "clippity, cloppity" sounds. I was the champion at making hoofbeats sounds, snapping my tongue back and forth across my upper lip. In fact, I can still do it. It *really* sounds good after I've had two glasses of wine.

Just because we had no horses didn't mean we didn't wear spurs. We made our own from tin cans. You laid the tin can on the ground and pounded the center of the can with the heel of your shoe until the ends of the can curled up and clamped onto the shoe. With a squashed can on each heel you clanked around just like a real cowboy. Except one day I couldn't get the "spurs" off my shoes. I didn't want to tell my mother about it because they were my good school shoes. I finally left them on the porch with the tin cans still attached when I went into the house for supper.

"Where are your shoes?" my mother asked.

"Uh . . . gee . . . I dunno, Ma."

"What do you mean you don't know? Nobody loses the shoes on their feet. You left here with shoes, and you'd better go and find them."

I finally had to come clean and show her the shoes. That was the end of my spurs.

In 1944 we moved to Milwaukee, and my cowboy days came to an abrupt end because there weren't any theaters in our new neighborhood that showed westerns. All of the big-city kids were playing war, so I became a soldier.

Jeff, however, continued the cowboy games back in Ishpeming. One afternoon he and another kid decided that they were going to go into a saloon, just like big cowboys did in the movies. The two of them went into the root cellar at Jeff's house where Jeff's old man had brewed and stored several bottles of homemade chokecherry wine. Using real shot glasses that they'd found in the kitchen upstairs, they poured themselves several quick ones and tossed them down.

Later on Jeff's mother noticed that her young cowboy was very green around the gills and went and got the doctor. That was back in the days when doctors still made house calls.

"He's been really sick, doctor," his mother said. "Is there any medicine I can give him?"

The doctor shook his head and closed his black bag. "Black coffee. Give him some black coffee. He's drunk."

Shortly afterward, by popular demand, Jeff also retired from the cowboy business.

&)CR

THE GREAT DEPRESSION SYNDROME

In one corner of my spare bedroom I have a humongous stash of cardboard boxes—all shapes and sizes—a pile so large that it eclipses the light from the window. When I started my own publishing company, I began saving boxes for shipping book orders. But most of the boxes in this pile are either too big or too small for shipping books because I've totally lost control. I now save every box I get my hands on. It's the Great-Depression Syndrome.

Depression babies like myself were taught the fundamentals of saving right from birth. My parents saved everything. In the 1930's and early '40's people didn't throw anything away because—and this was the catch phrase of the Depression era—someday you might need it, you never know.

Back then, purchases at J.C. Penny, or any other store, were always wrapped in brown paper and tied with white string. People saved the paper and string because, well . . . you never know. Of course, the stores provided a lot more string than anyone needed, but people saved it anyway, winding the string into large balls. Truly dedicated string savers had balls one or two feet in diameter. That's why kite flying was so popular when I was a kid. We had to do something with all of that string.

The meat market wrapped our pork chops in pink butcher

paper—thicker and of a much higher quality than the paper from J.C. Penny. I wiped the blood from the butcher paper and saved it to draw pictures on. Picasso had his Blue Period; I had my Pink Period.

People saved tinfoil. I remember meticulously peeling tinfoil from empty Lucky Strike and Phillip Morris packs that I found in the alley behind our house. Like the string, people saved it in a ball. I never did figure out what to use the tinfoil for, but I saved it anyway.

My old man saved old inner tubes, and he never even owned a car. I was the only one in the family who found a use for them. Sliced up inner-tube rubber came in handy for making ski binders, slingshots, and rubber guns. If you don't know what a rubber gun is, drop me a line and I'll send you a blueprint.

Gold Medal and Pillsbury were always in hot competition to see who could market the prettiest flour sacks, because women used them to make dresses. One company—I don't remember which—did very well by packing their grape jelly in fancy jars. People used the jelly jars as drinking glasses. One summer I got absolutely sick of grape jelly just because my mother wanted to get a matching set.

My mother also had a huge collection of buttons that she had rescued from worn-out clothes and kept in a jar the size of a goldfish bowl. Whenever anybody lost a button from a shirt or coat she'd scatter the button collection across the living-room rug and paw through them until she found a close match.

My father, with his team of draft horses, hauled garbage for the A&P store in Ishpeming. Not everything made it to the dump, though. He'd bring home the wooden produce crates for kindling. But before they were stuck in the stove it was my job to pull all of the nails from the crates and straighten them out for future use. In fact, at the tender age of eight, I was a pretty fair backyard carpenter, building a hideout on the back of our house out of vegetable-crate lumber.

Everything got used and reused. People nailed pop-bottle caps onto boards to make storm-porch boot scrapers. They washed out paper drinking straws and used them again and again. After each New Year's Day I had to carefully take the tinsel icicles off the Christmas tree, straighten them out, and put them back into the box for use next Christmas. I don't have to tell you what we did with old Sears and Roebuck catalogs (the black and white pages were much softer than the colored glossies). At one time or another my mother darned and patched every piece of clothing we owned—shirts, pants, socks, and underwear. And when the clothes just got too raggedy to repair, they were cut into strips and woven into carpets. People saved rain water because it was softer than what came out of the faucet, much better for scrubbing the threadbare clothes.

The mind boggles to think what would have happened if, back in the '30's, people'd had access to some of our more recent innovations. Ziploc bags would have been absolute treasures, washed, pressed, and put away with the good dishes—maybe even given as Christmas presents. Bubble Wrap would have made excellent mackinaw lining. I probably would have carefully peeled the shrink-wrap plastic film from everything, saved it in a great big ball, and put it next to the string and tinfoil because, well . . . you never know.

⊰⊱

RETHINKING MODERN MEDICINE

The other day my doctor gave me a prescription to treat a gastric disturbance (I'll spare you the details). A pharmacist's computer printout came with the capsules stating that this drug may cause nausea, blurred vision, weakness, lowered blood pressure, muscle cramps, headache, rash, swelling of the hands and feet, and constipation.

My heart began pounding; my hands got clammy; I broke into a cold sweat. I felt worse than I did before seeing the doctor. Would I have to get another medication to battle the side effects?

Staying healthy at my age is a tough, ongoing process. Everything in my body needs to be raised, lowered, bypassed, thinned, enriched, or redistributed. I take B-12 to raise my energy level, Lipitor to lower my cholesterol, aspirin to thin my blood, and if I remember to take it, ginkgo biloba to improve my memory. You know those plastic pill containers with separate compartments for every day of the week? Mine is the fancy model with multiple compartments for each day. Some pills I take in the morning, then a few with dinner, and finally a batch at bedtime. On Sunday mornings I spend fifteen minutes loading this thing up. I have to stack the pills in very carefully, otherwise they won't fit. I need a bigger pill box.

Going to doctors is even worse. The first thing they want to see is a complete record of every measurable parameter of my body. After scanning the readouts the doctor usually suggests that I see a specialist. The specialist often recommends that I see a more specialized specialist. Do these guys play golf together and hatch these plots on the nineteenth hole?

My parents never believed in pills, shots, or doctors. During my entire childhood I saw a doctor twice: the day I was born and when I had the chickenpox at age seven. Dr. McCann of Ishpeming made the house call both times. (How many of you remember doctors making house calls?) During the chickenpox visit the doctor looked me over, told my mother to keep me quiet and in bed, and then nailed a very large "QUARANTINE" sign on our door. My mother didn't think he'd said anything about chickenpox that she didn't already know, and she really didn't appreciate the quarantine sign, so Dr. McCann was never invited back.

When I was small I used to get earaches. My mother was convinced that camphorated oil was just the thing for that. She'd heat it up in a pan on the stove, grab me, jerk my head sideways, and pour the steaming oil into my ear. It was like a medieval torture. I screamed and hollered, but apparently it worked. My inner ear was frightened into wellness.

I used to get childhood headaches, too, but I was never given aspirin. My old man, a self-taught, amateur chiropractor, had the perfect cure. He'd grab my head with both hands, one on top of my skull and the other under my jaw, and with one swift wrenching motion twist my head 180 degrees, snapping and cracking every bone in my neck. The process was violent and terrifying, but like the camphorated oil, it did the job.

For everything else my mother liberally dosed me with cod-liver oil, a toxic substance with the color and viscosity of motor oil and a taste to match. Here again it was apparently instrumental in getting me through kidhood in relatively good health.

But as soon as I left home, I became exposed to modern medicine. At age eighteen I was getting a freshman physical at the University of Michigan, standing buck naked in a mile-long line of males on the running track in one of the university's gymnasiums while fuzzy-faced medical interns looked us over.

With no clothes on we all looked alike, buttocks gleaming under the fluorescent lights, except that I was unique in one respect. I'd never been stuck with a needle in my life.

A young intern looked over my medical questionnaire form. "I think you made a mistake here. You claim you've never had a shot or vaccination."

"That's right."

"No smallpox, diphtheria, not even a tetanus shot?"

"Nothing."

The intern couldn't believe his good luck. He gleefully yelled out to one of his white-coated associates, "Brad, grab the needles! We got a virgin here . . . never been stuck!"

So here I am, fifty years later, and I've been measured, probed, jabbed, stabbed, sliced, and diced by half the medical profession in the country. I've had enough X-rays fired into me to become radioactive. I've spent countless hours waiting in frigid examining rooms dressed in nothing but a paper mini-dress with no back. The doctor's bills I've run up in my lifetime would finance a Lear jet. Yet, I'm not nearly as healthy as I was when I was a kid, and don't tell me that it's old age, because right now I should be in the prime of life. At least according to my AARP magazines.

My father lived to be eighty-nine, and my mother passed away quietly in her sleep at ninety-five, and they shunned pills and doctors most of their lives. Maybe I should go over to Wal-Mart and see if I can find some of that cod-liver oil. It couldn't hurt.

∞⳥

REMEMBERING 1942

Memory can become slippery with age. Many times I'd driven past the old, abandoned gas station on the corner of Cleveland and Third Street in downtown Ishpeming, yet it was only the other day as I was going by, that something finally tweaked my brain.

"My gawd," I blurted to myself. "That used to be Mecca's Shell station!"

The reason that I remember this less-than-distinguished landmark was the bomb shelter beneath it. In early 1942 the country was gearing up for another fierce and bloody world war. U.S. forces were retreating in the South Pacific. German and Japanese submarines were prowling around off our coasts. Those were grim days. Everyone thought that American cities might be bombed at any moment. But Mecca Quayle was prepared for the worst. At his little Shell station on Cleveland and Third he'd converted a subterranean room under the service-station office into a bomb shelter. Mecca hadn't made the shelter public knowledge, but my father knew about it. The old man used to hang around the gas station in the evenings with the rest of Mecca's cronies, smoking cigarettes, drinking coffee, and chewing the rag. One night after supper he took me along.

I couldn't believe my good luck when Mecca let me climb down into the bomb shelter. To a nine-year-old boy a war was hugely exciting, but being able to go into an honest-to-goodness bomb shelter was the next best thing to going overseas with a rifle.

The shelter had everything necessary to sit out an air raid: an iron cot, wooden folding chairs, plenty of canned Spam and peaches, large maps of Europe and the South Pacific on the walls, and most importantly, a radio. Once I became a member of Mecca's inner circle, my father and I joined the group of men descending the narrow stairs into the bomb shelter every evening after supper to listen to the war news. The air in the stuffy little room turned blue with cigarette smoke as we huddled around the big wooden radio while Gabriel Heater and Walter Winchell gloomily broadcast the day's events. All the while Mecca would move little Nazi and Japanese flags around on the maps, depicting the latest front-line movements.

After the news I'd rush home. On my bedroom walls I had similar maps, and I'd quickly replant my own flags to maintain current accuracy. My walls were also adorned with a complete set of aircraft-spotter silhouettes of every known German and Japanese fighter plane and bomber. If we were going to be under attack, I wanted to be ready.

The war had an immediate impact on everyone's daily lives. All types of rationing went into effect. Coffee was in very limited supply and required ration stamps. Hard-core coffee drinkers made do by adding boiling water to the same coffee grounds over and over again until the brew became so thin that you could read a newspaper through it. This "Roosevelt coffee," as some called it, certainly didn't keep anyone awake at night.

Butter was unavailable. In its place was oleomargarine, not the tasty stuff you buy today at the supermarket, but a white, pasty, lardlike substance that even *tasted* like lard. Manufacturers tried to pacify the public by supplying a yellow color berry along with each pound. The color had to be mixed into the oleo to make it at least *look* like butter. It didn't help much.

Car owners were allowed three gallons of gasoline a week. They received a small square "A" sticker that had to be displayed on the corner of the windshield. Folks who could justify using their auto for business purposes got more gasoline and a "B" sticker for their windshield. "C" stickers were for those able to wield unlimited clout with the powers that be. You didn't see too many of those around Ishpeming.

Once a week all of the kids in our third-grade class bought savings stamps from the teacher—ten cents for a red stamp or twenty-five cents for a blue one (only the rich kids in north Ishpeming could afford the blue stamps). The stamps were pasted into a book, and when the book was filled it was worth $18.75 and turned in for a war bond. Years later those war bonds got me through my senior year at the University of Michigan.

Before the war kids had been scouring Ishpeming's back alleys for empty bottles to sell to local bootleggers to scrape up enough money for the Saturday matinee. When the war started, scrap iron became the commodity of choice. There was no money in it for us kids; we were just patriotic zealots. We had scrap-iron races to see who could amass the largest pile in our backyards. It got so bad that we even resorted to stealing scrap iron from each other.

From now on, every time I drive by that old gas station I'll cherish the memories of those bleak but exciting times in 1942. Now that I think about it though, a gasoline station wasn't exactly the ideal site for a bomb shelter, but then again Ishpeming wasn't exactly a prime enemy target, so I suppose it was okay.

„›•‘”

MISSION IMPOSSIBLE—LEARNING FINNISH

On the Fourth of July I was signing books at the Annual Finnish Music Festival in Covington, a very nice event with a large crowd of friendly people, plenty of good food and drink, and lively music (you can always attract Finns with beer, pasties, and polkas). Very enjoyable, except for one little thing. Every now and then a Finn person would walk up to my book table, glance at my name on the banner, and say:

"Jerry Harju—hyvää päivää?"

Being of Finnish descent, I of course knew what was said (loose translation: how do you do?). But I just returned the greeting with "Pretty good, thanks" in English. If I answered with "Kiitos, hyvin," they'd want to continue the conversation in Finn, and then I'd really be up the creek.

I never learned to speak Finnish, although both of my parents and my older sister, Esther, spoke it fluently. To this day I maintain that my mother and father elected not to teach me so they could hold private conversations in Finn whenever I was within earshot. Years later I accused my mother of this conspiracy, but she vehemently denied it, claiming that I just wasn't smart enough to pick up the language.

She may have been right. Finnish is one of the most

incomprehensible languages on the face of the earth. It doesn't sound like any language you've ever heard. It bears no relationship to English whatsoever, nor does it even faintly resemble Spanish, Italian, or German. The Finnish alphabet has letters missing and others added (ä and ö). There are no articles. *Talo* means both "a house" and "the house." The words are extremely long and liberally laced with diphthongs—double vowels with each pronounced separately. I know all this may sound picky, but it's a very strange, tough language. At one time I learned Spanish, and that was dirt simple compared to Finnish.

Of course, during my childhood I couldn't help but pick up a few Finnish words, mostly food: *maito*, milk; *leipä*, bread; *voita*, butter. One that never escaped my young eardrums was *jää kerma*, ice cream. Before going grocery shopping at the A&P, my mother and father would often discuss buying ice cream as a surprise treat for me, furtively speaking in Finn so I wouldn't pick up on it. But I quickly learned the word (I wasn't quite as dumb as my mother thought) and would excitedly yell out what flavor I wanted.

Many years ago I made a concerted effort to learn Finn. It was before a trip to Finland with Roger Roney, a friend of mine. For two months prior to the trip I played a Finnish language cassette over and over while driving back and forth to work in Los Angeles, startling other drivers at red lights with my counting aloud in Finnish:

"Yksi . . . kaksi . . . kolme . . . neljä . . . viisi . . ."

When Roger and I reached Finland we rented a car at the airport and began threading our way through downtown Helsinki, looking for our hotel. I was driving and Roger was navigating. In addition to having the world's toughest language, Finland has street names that will put your jaw in traction. Our hotel was supposed to be located on a street called Pohjoisesplanadi (don't ask me to pronounce it), a block down from Aleksanterinkatu, just off the main thoroughfare of Mannerheimintie. To make matters worse, the street signs have teeny, tiny print, in both Finnish and Swedish, a concession to the Swedes who had earlier invaded Finland.

Roger glanced frantically back and forth between the map on his lap and the minuscule street signs, moving his lips as he tried to read off the long names.

"You say we're looking for . . . P . . . o . . .h . . .j . . .?"

"Yeah, yeah, that's the one. Is it this street?"

"No, it was four blocks back."

We finally found the hotel, and the next morning we began driving north on our Finland adventure. I was supremely confident of my newly acquired mastery of Finnish, at least to handle the two most important things necessary for survival—ordering coffee and asking where the toilet was. The food on the restaurant menus was a little beyond my Finnish language skills, so Roger and I would often just point at something on the menu and hope for the best. However, I knew that with constant practice my Finnish would dramatically improve before the trip was over.

But throughout the trip every Finn that we met in hotels, restaurants, and gas stations would take one gander at our clothes and the new cameras around our necks and immediately begin speaking to us in English. Frustrated at not having the opportunity to practice my Finnish, I finally used it on an unsuspecting hotel desk clerk in Rovaniemi.

"Haw-loo-aw-seen hooo-a-nayn yo-assah own soo-koo." I was attempting to say: I want a room with a shower.

My Finnish startled the desk clerk, and he nervously edged away from me, desperately looking around for assistance from his co-workers.

"I thought I'd phrased that pretty well," I said to Roger who was standing next to me, quietly snickering.

"He probably thinks you're speaking Russian, and you might be a secret agent reconnoitering another Soviet invasion," Roger replied.

When I returned to Los Angeles I could find no Finns to practice on, and over the years I lost what little Finnish I had acquired. So if you're a Finn and you should see me signing books somewhere, go easy, it's not like I haven't tried.

ഇറ

"NUMBER, PLEASE"

Not long ago I was sitting, reading quietly, in the Detroit Metro Airport, waiting for the Northwest puddle-jumper to Marquette. I looked up from my book and observed the phenomenon of our time—six people nearby, all talking on cell phones.

People are no longer content to merely sit, stand, or drive anymore; they have to be talking on their cell phone at the same time. They carry these tiny phones in pockets or purses to ward off withdrawal symptoms. They kill themselves on highways, dialing with their hands and steering with their knees. Telephones are now everywhere. You can buy them for next to nothing at Wal-Mart or Shopko so you can have at least three in every room in the house.

When I was a kid, right up through high school, my family never had a telephone. But we muddled along just fine. If we wanted to talk to someone, we wrote a letter or hiked over to their house. I was eight years old—living in Ishpeming—before I even *saw* my first telephone. My pal, Jimmy Sharland, came up to me in school and proudly announced that his family had just gotten a phone. After school I rushed over to his house to take a look at it.

Telephones in those days looked like long-necked birds dressed in black (telephones only came in black for many years). You spoke into the bird's mouth while holding the bell-shaped receiver to your ear. These "hook and ladder" phones, as they were called, had no dials or buttons. As soon as you took the receiver from its cradle, a little bulb would light up on an operator's switchboard somewhere, and she would come on the line to connect you to your party.

I stood there in awe, staring at Jimmy's new telephone. I'd seen telephones in movies where Fred Astaire and other grand people living in penthouses had them, but I never thought I'd ever be standing next to one.

Jimmy grinned and pointed to the receiver. "Go 'head, I doubledare ya t'pick it up."

A doubledare was not something to be taken lightly, so I carefully removed the receiver from its cradle, and Jimmy and I both listened. We giggled when the operator said, "Number, please."

Then she said in a stern voice, "You kids will have to get off the telephone. Only grownups are supposed to use it."

My grandparents in Republic were the first in our family to get a telephone. I was staying with them during the summer of 1947 when my Uncle Arvid had one installed in their living room. It made for high excitement. Neighbors and relatives invented any excuse to come over just to see if the phone would ring. The telephone number was only three digits, but that was plenty. The directory for the whole town of Republic was only a half-page long.

My grandfather loved that telephone. But his friends didn't have phones, so he would call Vierela's grocery store in Republic on the pretext of checking on the availability of rusk toast or whatever. At the top of his voice he would yell in Finn into the phone at Fred Vierela, and sitting in the living room I could hear Fred yelling back. They didn't need a phone at all. All they would've had to do was stick their heads out the window.

Republic had its own telephone switchboard—I don't remember where it was—but the operator knew everyone in town personally.

Before she connected you with your party she would ask how you were feeling or how your ailing mother was doing. But in the evening she closed up the switchboard and went home, and that was pretty much it for the telephone service in Republic until the next morning when she opened it up again.

In the early days there were party lines, which meant that you shared the same telephone line with three or four other people. You knew who the call was for by the number of rings. Before television, one of the major sources of home entertainment was listening in on other people's calls. You had to have the finger dexterity of a safecracker in order to lift the receiver off the cradle without the people on the line hearing the telltale click.

When I was attending the University of Michigan in Ann Arbor in the '50's, my mother was always after me to write home. I hated writing letters though, and every so often I'd scrape up a handful of nickels and dimes and call home from a pay phone.

"Hi, Ma, it's me."

My mother would get very alarmed. No one called long distance unless it was an emergency.

She'd yell into the phone, "What's wrong?"

"Nothing's wrong, Ma. I just thought I'd talk to you."

"What's this phone call costing you?"

"I don't know, Ma, but don't worry. I can afford it."

"It wouldn't hurt to write a letter once in awhile and save your money for books," she'd say.

I'm convinced that what goes around will come around. With this new, fancy speech-recognition circuitry, phones again won't need buttons or dials. You'll simply wave your hand over the instrument and a computerized voice will say, "Number, please." It'll be a nice reminiscent touch, but I'll bet it won't ask you how your ailing mother is doing.

₧₨

RIDING THE TIN GOOSE

When I was a kid I had a passion for airplanes. I laboriously carved models of the Flying Fortress and British Spitfire out of balsa wood, collected airmail stamps, and took in all the airplane movies I could afford. Every time I spotted an open-cockpit biplane soaring over Ishpeming, I yearned to be up there, decked out in a flashy leather helmet and large goggles, a gloved hand on the joy stick, grinning as I leaned over to gaze down at the ant-sized people in Ishpeming.

One day in 1940, when I was seven years old, a friend of my father—one of the rare people who owned a car—came over and asked if we wanted to take a ride with him to the Marquette airport to see a big airplane.

I squealed with delight. The three of us piled into the old Chevy coupe and took off for the airport. It wasn't hard to find the airplane because there was a huge crowd gathered at the airport fence, gawking. In those days there weren't many airplanes in the U.P.

The Ford Tri-Motor sat there, the pilot revving up the three powerful engines. The draft from the propellers swirled the runway grass in dizzying circles. The first time I'd seen an airplane up close. I was totally captivated.

They were offering rides for fifty cents a person. I jumped up and down and begged my father to let me go on the airplane. The old man looked at me, amazed.

"Where' th'hell ya think I'm gonna get fifty cents?" People were still struggling through the final days of the Depression. He added, "If I had fifty cents, I'd go for a ride myself!" The old man loved airplanes, too.

I was heartbroken, but there was no point in further discussion. I lost my chance to ride in the Ford Tri-Motor.

Until now. The other day I heard that a 1929 Ford Tri-Motor was landing at the Sawyer airport, again offering rides to the public. I rushed out there. Sixty years later I was getting a second chance.

Ford Motor Company built a total of 199 Tri-Motors from 1926 until production was stopped in 1933. It was one of the earliest commercial airliners built. With a fuel capacity of 235 gallons, the airplane, affectionately nicknamed the "Tin Goose," had the astounding range of 500 miles and could carry nine passengers.

Eastern Air Transport—the forerunner of Eastern Airlines—bought several Tri-Motors and launched an advertising campaign claiming that they could take you "Coast to Coast in 48 Hours!" But it wasn't your typical coast-to-coast air travel. The plane would take off from California in the morning, ferrying its passengers eastward during the daylight hours, landing several times throughout the day to refuel. The plane wasn't designed for night operation and had to make its final landing of the day at sundown. The travelers then boarded a train, retiring into Pullman cars for the night while the train continued the eastward journey. In the morning the adventurous (and wealthy, I might add) airline passengers would board yet another Ford Tri-Motor and travel east in this fashion until they reached New York City two days later. Not exactly a commuter flight.

I was eagerly waiting at Sawyer Airport when the Tri-Motor arrived. It looked smaller than I remembered it in 1940, but I was impressed all the same. The plane has three nine-cylinder radial engines, one mounted under each wing with the third in the fuselage nose. The wingspan—seventy-four feet—is enormous for the airplane's overall size. In the 1930's you needed big wings in case the engines quit—which they often did—and you had to glide to earth.

The Tin Goose has other unusual features. The cables for the rudder and elevator control surfaces are attached to the outside of the fuselage, which would make for a real dodgy operation in a U.P. ice storm. Gauges for the two outboard engines are located right above the engines themselves, forcing the pilot to look out the window to check the oil pressure. He'd have to use a flashlight at night. There are no wing flaps at all.

I thought, do I really want to leave the ground in this thing? The plane is an antique! It's older than I am!

I climbed into the airplane. The inside cabin was quite small, but luxurious by 1929 standards, with wood cabin paneling, comfortable brown leather seats with more legroom than today's airliners, and stout overhead netting for your carry-on luggage. You'd best visit the bathroom before you leave the house and also take along a heavy jacket, because the Tin Goose lacks certain amenities, like heat and a toilet.

The plane quickly filled up with passengers, but the pilot was still seated in the cockpit all by himself. He turned to us in the main cabin. "I need a copilot up here. Any volunteers?"

I about popped a disk jumping out of my seat and scrambling up the narrow aisle into the cockpit. Before he changed his mind I quickly plopped myself into the right-hand copilot's seat and buckled up.

The pilot, handed me a heavy-duty headset. "Put this on. It'll cut down on the noise."

He had that right. With all three engines cranked up and the fuselage engine only a few feet in front of my knees, the noise was deafening, even with the headset clamped tightly over my ears.

We taxied out to the Sawyer runway. I idly wondered if the pilot had really been looking for a bona fide co-pilot when he made the announcement.

I tapped him on the shoulder, pointing toward the open cockpit window on my side, wanting to know when I should slide it shut.

His voice crackled into my headset. "Leave it open. That's our air conditioning."

We got tower clearance for takeoff, and the pilot pushed all three engine throttles forward. With tooth-rattling vibration and noise, the Tin Goose surged forward, straining to achieve its takeoff airspeed of 65 MPH. But with its huge wings the old Tri-Motor leapt off the runway within a hundred yards of our starting point. A wedge shot for Tiger Woods.

We chugged up to an altitude of two-thousand feet and at a lightning-fast cruising speed of 85 MPH proceeded north toward Marquette, low enough for the passengers to enjoy the brilliant fall colors on the trees.

It was over all too quickly. Much sooner than I wished, we returned to the airport, and the old airplane floated down and lightly touched the Sawyer runway.

I wondered if the old man, wherever he is, was watching, knowing that I'd finally realized my sixty-year-old dream. I hoped so. Of course, he was probably jealous.

80G3

"TRICKY" HALLOWEENS

The other day my friend Jeff and I were having lunch at Peggy Sue's Cafe in Ishpeming, slurping up the addictive pea soup while we hashed over the usual topics totally outside of our control—the weather, old age, and women. Then—I suppose because it's October—we got onto the subject of Halloween.

"Kids today come up to your door and yell 'Trick or Treat,' but they don't even know what that means," Jeff commented. "Halloween tricks are ancient history." He grinned fiendishly. "Remember what we used to do?"

I nodded with a grin. "I remember."

When we were kids, Halloween trick or treating was precisely that. If people didn't cough up treats for the pint-sized ghosts and goblins on the doorstep, they were on the receiving end of some really rotten tricks. It was pure and simple blackmail. Grownups who didn't lay in a good supply of Tootsie Rolls, malted-milk balls, or licorice sticks suffered instant retaliation.

Wax was the primary weapon. We used it on windows and windshields of anyone who didn't fork over goodies at the front door. Waxing house windows was a hazardous endeavor, though. It required a delicate, surgeon-like touch to avoid detection, because if you inadvertently rattled the window, some burly bozo sitting in the living room would hear you and dash out and kick your butt up between your ears. Jeff came up with a foxy approach to minimize the risk. He borrowed a clothes pole from the backyard, tied a candle to the end, and waxed the upstairs windows while everyone in the house was still downstairs.

I was partial to rocks inside automobile hubcaps. The day after Halloween, people carefully steered their rattling heaps down to the mechanic, convinced that the car had serious drive shaft or rear-end problems.

Another favorite was collecting doggy poop in a paper bag, setting it on fire on a doorstep, then knocking on the door and diving into the bushes to watch the flaming bag get stomped out by an unsuspecting foot.

Halloween tricks also served as payback for injustices. One old curmudgeon who lived in the Salisbury location in Ishpeming was always yelling at kids who cut across his yard. Naturally, his outhouse was regularly tipped over every Halloween. Seeking revenge, the old guy snuck into his privy early one Halloween eve to wait for the kids, intending to pound on any he could catch. Unfortunately, he fell asleep. Later that night the outhouse got flipped over with him inside. It landed on the door, and he only escaped by squeezing out through the business hole.

For several years I cleverly pulled off Halloween pranks without getting caught. I waxed windows and rocked hubcaps with professional aplomb, convinced that I was smarter and more cunning than any bumbling adult who ineffectively attempted to guard his property on Halloween night.

Then came October, 1945. I was laboring through the seventh grade in Republic, under the brutal iron thumb of an evil teacher whose name shall be withheld. For purposes of this narrative I'll refer to her as the Old Witch, although we substituted another letter for the "W."

She assigned humongous amounts of homework and kept us after school for the most trivial infractions. And she was not above using physical force in the classroom. As Halloween approached, my mind turned to thoughts of payback.

One afternoon, a week before Halloween, I was poking around in the Republic dump, looking for good stuff, as was my custom in those days. I came across a practically full, thirty-pound sack of flour.

I would have cried out "Eureka!" if I had known the word, but instead I yelled "That's it!" and grabbed the sack of flour and lugged it home.

Late on Halloween night I skulked over to the Old Witch's house with the sack of flour. The house was dark, indicating that she had already gone to bed. I diligently set about my task, quickly sprinkling the flour all over her front lawn.

This subversive activity attracted no one's attention, and it would have been the perfect crime except that I went too far. I capped off the operation by scrawling a few low-brow taunting remarks on the side of her garage, using lipstick which I'd also found in the dump.

The next morning, on the way to school, I walked past her house to inspect my handiwork. She had gotten up early and had already scrubbed the lipstick off the garage wall. But the lawn was a different story. The heavy morning dew had transformed the dusting of flour into paste, clinging fast to the grass like a coat of plaster. I'd pulled off another brilliant Halloween trick.

I was feeling pretty smug sitting at my desk as the school day began. However, instead of chalking up the usual early morning arithmetic problems on the blackboard, the Old Witch told everyone to place their hands on the desk, palms up.

Puzzled, I looked down at my hands. Imbedded in the creases were very visible traces of red lipstick.

The teacher stared down at my hands and froze me with a malevolent icy stare. She knew. And she knew that I *knew* she knew.

I spent all that day and the days to follow, cringing with fear at my desk, waiting for the ax to fall. But the Old Witch didn't say or do a thing. She elected to employ the cruelest punishment of all—anticipation. The condemned man never feels the firing-squad's bullets but dies a thousand deaths standing at the wall waiting.

So that was my Halloween-trick swan song. Realizing that adults can be a bit smarter than kids, I hung up my wax, rocks, doggy-poop bags, and flour and retired from the game.

ഌരു

BUCKLE UP AND SLOW DOWN

I had an auto accident the other day. For thirty-eight years I effortlessly zoomed up and down Los Angeles freeways without so much as a fender scratch. Now I'm living in Marquette, Michigan, where the morning rush hour amounts to three cars in a row going down Washington Street, and I somehow manage to smack up the front end of my Chevy Lumina.

I was on the curved connector road joining South Front Street with US-41 in Marquette, on my way to Ishpeming to a book signing. The roadway was coated with the usual Upper Michigan wintertime slush mixed with sand and salt. I'll admit that I was traveling a wee bit too fast. The next thing I knew I was moving briskly eastward on US-41 . . . sideways. I twisted the steering wheel—I don't even remember which way—and talk about power steering, the wheel seemed to be connected to thin air. My Yooper driving skills completely deserted me, and I committed the worst sin imaginable during a spin; I put on the brakes. The corkscrewing Chevy actually picked up speed and headed toward the divider rail.

The front end of the car crashed into the rail with a resounding bang, not hard enough to activate the air bag but enough to rattle my eyeballs and make me a lifelong advocate of seat belts which kept me from wearing the steering wheel for the rest of the day.

I wasn't hurt, only stunned. Then I realized that the car was sitting crosswise in the fast lane with traffic bearing down on me. I quickly rammed the Chevy into reverse and snaked it over to the shoulder. I tried to get the driver's door open, but it was jammed so I squirmed over to the passenger side and scrambled out.

The so-called bumper—they aren't designed for bumps anymore—had a bad dent, the hood looked sprung, and the left front fender had been pushed back enough to pinch the driver's door in the closed position. It wasn't a bad collision, but when these new cars travel any faster than walking speed and hit something, they buckle like tinfoil.

As luck would have it, an off-duty police officer behind me saw the whole thing and called it in on his mobile phone. Another patrolman showed up and took down all the information. The car was drivable, and I headed on my way, thanking the Man Upstairs that it hadn't been worse.

My near-perfect driving record goes back further than my California days. The only other accident I've had was in 1949 when I was learning how to drive. I was a high-school sophomore in Republic, bubbling over with testosterone, and intent on embarking on a lifelong career of picking up girls and cruising. But since I still didn't have a driver's license, I was forced to rely on my older adolescent cronies who did.

One evening Melvin (a.k.a. Sluggo) Poylio picked me up in his old man's Ford pickup truck. We set about our usual nightly mission of picking up a couple of girls and hotrodding around. After a few false starts we got lucky with two cuties. The girls squeezed into the cab between Sluggo and me, and we began the second phase of the mission: showing the girls how fast the truck would go.

Sluggo put on a superb driving clinic outside of town, spraying gravel in all directions as he skillfully negotiated hairpin turns on the narrow roads. Then it was my turn. There was no Driver's Education in those days, so you had to take every opportunity to practice on back roads. I eagerly got behind the wheel and stomped on the gas petal.

On the second or third curve I lost it. The truck, going much too fast, slid into a roadside ditch and turned over on its side.

For a moment we sat there, one on top of another, in a state of shock. The truck was resting on its right side, so I was sprawled on top, the two girls in the middle, and Sluggo trapped on the bottom. I tried to open the driver's door above me, but it was too heavy. Lying on my side against a cute girl, I had no leverage to lift it.

Finally Sluggo said, "We better get outta here before the truck catches on fire."

The girls rendered immediate assistance. With yelps of panic they somehow got to their feet inside the cab—stepping on Sluggo's face in the process—and threw me bodily up and out of the driver's door.

We finally got the truck upright and back into town. The Ford had a sizable dent in the right front fender, and Sluggo and I decided to do the repair so his old man wouldn't see it. We brought the truck to the Standard station where we put it up on the hoist, removed the right front wheel, and took a ball-peen hammer to the inside of the fender to pound out the dent. Now, instead of one big dent, the fender had many small dents, like a bad case of goosebumps.

Aside from some miscellaneous traffic tickets over the years, this is a complete history of my driving record. So have a safe and sane New Year, folks. Just remember, buckle up and slow down. The life you save may be mine.

ഏറൽ

MARBLES, KNIVES, AND OTHER RITES OF SPRING

W hen I was a kid, the final meltdown of the familiar old gray snowbanks in our neighborhood was the signal for a host of pastimes to replace ski-jumping, sledding, and snowball wars.

The first thing we got into as soon as the dirt firmed up was marbles. In Ishpeming we had a special game of marbles called "pot marbles." (I haven't seen or heard of it since.) A three-inch-diameter hole—the pot—was dug in the dirt, and a line was drawn some eight feet away. We'd stand behind the line and pitch marbles at the pot. If yours was the closest marble, you took the first shot. You'd get on your knees in the dirt and plink the marble with your index finger, rolling it at the pot like a golf putt. For the first shot you'd select your own marble, which was the closest to the hole. If it went in, you got to shoot someone else's marble; otherwise, you gave up your turn. Since you kept the marbles you put into the pot, this was not at all a friendly game. Bitter shoving matches or even fistfights often resulted when a player lost his favorite marble to an opponent.

While most marbles were cheap colored glass, there was actually a wide range of quality. If I was up against some really hot shooters, I'd use clay marbles, about as worthless as rocks. Clay marbles were soft, often chipping, and sometimes even breaking in two, so it wasn't a big deal if you lost one in a match. The real prizes were "steelies." These were nothing but ball bearings but weren't easy for us to lay our hands on since they weren't sold at our favorite haunts. Steelies were a lot heavier than your average marble. Which was good because they didn't bounce all over the place when pitched at the pot. They came to earth with a righteous thud, staying right where they hit. This usually assured the crafty steelie owner the first shot. It took a strong finger to shoot a steelie, though, and you had to practice a lot.

In the fifth grade my friend Jeff experienced a tragic loss when a couple of precious steelies fell out of his pocket during arithmetic class and hit the floor with a loud crash and then rolled up to the head of the room. The teacher immediately confiscated them. Back then you could bring jackknives to school, but not marbles.

Speaking of jackknives, another springtime game we played after school was mumbletypeg, but we called it "Knives." The object of Knives was to execute a series of progressively-more-complicated jackknife flips, sticking the blade into the ground each time. You had to successfully complete each flip before going on to the next one. Soft dirt, even mud, was preferable so the blade would stick easily.

Each flip maneuver had a name, like "Hand," "Elbow," or "Knee." For example, to execute the "Hand" maneuver you'd carefully balance the tip of the jackknife blade on the back of your left hand, trying not to draw blood, of course. The knife was held upright with your right hand, and with this hand you'd flip the knife toward the ground so it would spin 360 degrees and stick in the dirt. For "Knee" you'd perch the knife blade on your left knee, doing primarily the same thing. If you were an inveterate Knives player, your whole left side was covered with scabby little knife-point pricks. Needless to say, Knives required a lot of practice, and every once in awhile a kid would run home to seek medical attention for a knife wound in his big toe.

The final game-winning flip was "Around the World" where

you'd place the jackknife flat in the open palm of your hand and toss it over your head, attempting to stick it in the ground behind you. I was never too good at Around the World, and every time I tried it the other Knives players always ducked for cover.

Springtime was also the season for making a new slingshot. Jeff and I would climb the bluff behind South Ishpeming, looking for the perfect slingshot crotch among the branches of young trees. A "U" crotch was preferable to a "V" but harder to find. We'd cut rubber strips from an old inner tube and tie them to the slingshot handle. Finally, we fashioned a pouch to hold the rock. Leather was best, so we'd use the tongue from an old shoe. Shoes were never thrown away until the tongues were removed.

And, of course, there was kite flying. I never had the foresight to save the lightweight tissue paper from my Christmas presents though it would have made excellent kite material. Instead I had to resort to using old *Mining Journal* newspaper or paper from the butcher shop, both heavy paper.

It wouldn't have made any difference, though, because I never truly grasped the art of kite flying. I deposited kites on roofs and in trees and snarled them around the tops of telephone poles. Other kids tried to help me, but it was no use. Years later, at the University of Michigan, I minored in aeronautical engineering, and I *still* don't think I'd be able to keep a kite in the air.

What do youngsters do in spring nowadays? I really don't know; I don't see many of them outside. Since jackknives and slingshots are strictly forbidden now—kids run the risk of expulsion if they're caught with them around school—I suppose they have to go home and content themselves with those video games where opponents are decapitated with laser weapons.

♧

MONTGOMERY WARD: A EULOGY

I couldn't believe it when I heard that Montgomery Ward was going out of business. It's like losing an old childhood friend.

When I was a kid, in the '30's and '40's, Montgomery Ward and Sears Roebuck were as essential as food and air. The arrival of their annual mail-order catalogs was an event rivaled only by Christmas. People would talk about the new catalogs weeks before they actually found their way into the mail box. Most of the merchandise was beyond everyone's means, but that was okay, they could dream. That's why the mail-order catalogs were called "wish books."

All year long my mother would spend evenings poring over the catalogs. She inspected the latest styles in women's clothes, looked at curtains, carpet sweepers, and kitchen stoves, and ogled diamond bracelets which she'd never own. My mother made a lot of her own clothes, and one thing she *could* afford were the dress patterns offered by Sears and Ward. She ordered a lot of those.

Men were no strangers to the catalogs either. There was always a fine selection of tools, boots, guns, and fishing gear. My father ordered a lot of stuff. One time he decided to repair our old alarm clock. He decided that we couldn't afford a new one, so he ordered a cheap watchmaker's tool kit from Ward. The only problem was that when he put the clock back together he had parts left over. Needless to say, the clock wouldn't run, and he finally had to order a new one from Ward.

The mail-order business catered to small farmers, mainly because there were so many of them in those days. Farmers could order almost anything they needed: cream separators, hog troughs, chicken feed, plows, corn huskers, cow dehorners, fertilizer spreaders, and windmills. I remember my father ordering new harnesses for his two draft horses from the Montgomery Ward catalog. I'll bet that's something you won't find on the Internet.

Why was mail order so popular? Because people couldn't travel any great distance to shop. Most folks, certainly the ones *we* knew, didn't have cars. Neither of my parents ever learned how to drive. If we somehow managed to get a ride to Marquette, it was a very big deal. Taking a trip to Milwaukee was like going to Europe. Chicago was as remote as the moon. So if we couldn't find whatever we needed in the small Ishpeming stores, it was time to reach for the mail-order catalog.

Sears Roebuck and Montgomery Ward had just about everything. You could order wallpaper, grindstones, sewing machines, wheelbarrows, meat grinders, Cuban cigars, pianos, milk bottles, hand-operated hair clippers, and sausage stuffers. Also, horse blankets, Japanese flower vases, lard presses, tombstones, and stoves that burned wood, coal, or corn cobs.

Ready for this? At one time Sears Roebuck sold a complete seven-room house for $2500.

If you were lucky enough to have a car, you probably repaired it yourself. All auto parts were available through Sears and Ward. Radiators, shock absorbers, water pumps, headlights, convertible tops, steering wheels, and complete engines. You could even buy fenders by mail order, although black was the only color available. Eighteen months was the longest guarantee you could get on a Sears car battery, but then they only cost about ten dollars. Those early mail-order tires were only guaranteed for fifteen thousand miles, so you ordered a tire-patching kit at the same time.

I can still remember the heart-stopping excitement of seeing the postman bringing a mail-order package that I'd ordered. My bicycle came from Sears. My very first baseball glove, a Hank Greenberg model, came from Montgomery Ward. When I was in high school in Republic, trapping weasels and muskrat, I bought my traps from the Sears catalog.

My most memorable catalog purchase was the shotgun I ordered from Montgomery Ward. It was a full-choke, twenty gauge single shot. The gun was inexpensive—about twelve dollars—mainly because it had a hollow plastic stock. The plastic made the shotgun very light, and it kicked like a mule when I fired it. I finally solved the problem by taking the base plate off the stock and stuffing it full of rags and pieces of scrap metal.

Finally, at the end of their twelve-month life span, the Ward and Sears catalogs always came to an inglorious, but useful end. They would be put in that little house down at the end of the path from the kitchen door, a place where one could sit and read, then use the pages for . . . well . . . other things. I think Montgomery Ward and Sears Roebuck had their customers comfort in mind when they made their catalogs with soft pages.

Rest in peace, Montgomery Ward. You leave fond memories.

ဆၵ

I WANT THE GOVERNMENT OUT OF MY BATHROOM

For the past two years I've been living in a nice apartment in Marquette—a spacious two-bedroom in an old refurbished mansion with a panoramic view of Lake Superior from my large, beamed-ceiling living room. A truly fantastic place that I intend to stay in for a long time.

There's only one problem. The toilet keeps stopping up.

Every day I assault the damned thing with my plumber's helper. Even that doesn't always do the trick, and I have to call the landlord. Each time he faithfully comes over with his plumber's snake and unplugs the beast.

One day when he'd finished the job, I asked him, "What keeps causing this?" I didn't tell him that my friend Jeff thinks the source of the problem is my affinity for All Bran.

"The toilet tank is too small," the landlord said.

I nodded but figured that he'd told me that only because he didn't want to think about a more major repair, like on the sewer line.

One day the toilet got seriously plugged when the landlord was out of town, and I had to call in a licensed plumber. He came in with his trusty snake and proceeded to do the same thing that my landlord had been doing all along.

"What keeps causing this?" I asked the plumber, thinking that now I'd get the straight poop (no pun intended).

"The toilet tank is too small," the plumber said.

"Too small?"

"Yep. Not enough water to do a good job of flushing."

"Well, I better talk the landlord into getting a toilet with a larger tank."

"No. Large-tank toilets are illegal now."

"Illegal? How can a toilet be illegal?"

The plumber went on to tell me that some years ago the federal government, in its infinite wisdom, passed an energy-conservation bill which, among other things, restricts the capacity of toilet tanks to 1.6 gallons. Old toilets had 3.5 gallon tanks which worked just fine, as I recall. If anyone now installs a 3.5 gallon toilet in their home, huge penalties are levied, I suppose, by the federal toilet police.

The reason for the bill was to conserve water. This is truly ironic because I have to flush the stupid thing three times to clear it, which, of course, soundly defeats water conservation. With these brave new toilets we're actually wasting water, not saving it. I think the whole ridiculous idea was foisted on Congress by lobbyists for the plunger industry.

As the plumber was leaving, he added, "You wouldn't have this problem if you lived in Canada. They still have the large-tank toilets."

That got me to thinking. What if I drove over to Sault Ste. Marie, Canada, bought a toilet (with untraceable cash, of course), put it in the trunk of my car, and drove back? I mean, it's not like smuggling heroin, is it?

Of course, I'd get very nervous facing the U.S. Customs agent at the border.

"How long have you been in Canada?"

"Oh, just today, sir. I was visiting my friend, Johnny."

"Are you bringing back any liquor or tobacco products?"

"Oh heavens no, sir. I would never bring in anything like that."

"Did you buy anything at all in Canada?"

"Oh, heh, heh, nothing much. Just a little porcelain souvenir. I think it's somewhere in the trunk."

But there could be serious jail time associated with toilet smuggling, so trying to get it by U.S. Customs might be very risky. A better plan would be to wait until winter and some night leave my car on the U.S. side, walk across the bridge, and then push the toilet across the ice on the St. Mary's River. I would imagine porcelain slides pretty well.

Of course, if the word gets out about these big Canadian toilets, everyone may start smuggling them in. U.S. Customs officials would be forced to use porcelain-sniffing dogs at the border.

Once I get the toilet home I'm sure I'd be able to find some fly-by-night plumber who'd come over to my place after dark in an unmarked van and install it for me. In the long run, I'd be serving the nation's needs by conserving water—only flushing once—and in the process I'd save my landlord a ton of money.

How did life become so complicated? When I was a kid in Republic, we had an outhouse. It may have been a trifle pungent in the summer, but I don't remember the government ever coming around and telling us how deep to dig the hole.

∞∞

MORE POOP ABOUT TOILETS

The big reader response to my toilet column really surprised me. It's depressing when the most popular piece I'd ever written is about a plugged-up potty. You might be interested in the latest developments.

First of all, nothing's changed at my place. I still conduct my early morning ritual with the trusty plunger, except that I'm becoming much more accomplished. I haven't had to call in the landlord or a professional plumber for months. It's probably my engineering background in fluid mechanics which has allowed me to scientifically analyze the problem. I'll skip over the technical details except to say that once the toilet handle is pulled, swift timing and wrist action are critical.

I've learned several things from readers who wrote in. Friends of mine from Michigamme, Cindy Coleman and Larry Shanley, said that while traveling through Canada around the north end of Lake Superior, they took the opportunity to look for a large-tank toilet to replace the one in their house. After crossing into Canada, Cindy went into the U.S. Customs office and asked if it was against the law to take a large Canadian toilet back into the U.S. The Customs people said that they had no orders to be the Toilet Police. In fact, one of them confided that he had planned to do the same thing. He was remodeling his house and had shopped around in Canada for a large toilet. Although Canadians don't have restrictions on toilet-tank capacity, all he could find for sale there were the U.S. toy toilets. Cindy and Larry didn't have any luck either. When it comes to toilets the Canadians don't seem to be any smarter than we are.

Exploring the subject further, I went over to Feltner Plumbing and Heating in Marquette. Jon, the manager, gave me some interesting information on the latest development in toilet technology. The Kohler company now puts out a new model which has a 3.5-gallon tank—REALLY big—but with factory settings on the linkage so that the amount of water flushed is limited to the federally mandated 1.6 gallons. However, it might not take much know-how to make a slight adjustment to, shall we say, improve the performance. (Are you following me here?)

A Japanese company puts out a model called Toto which is supposed to be the Top Gun in toilets. Toto has a 3-inch flush valve—much bigger than standard—which propels water into the bowl with such supersonic force that it will suck the towels right off the bathroom wall racks. I'd think twice about sitting on that baby while flushing.

At the end of the first column I made the rash comment that when I was a kid the government never told us how deep to dig the hole for our privy. Bill Pesola of Marquette sent me a copy of the state Environmental Health Code, pointing out that now the government—at least the state of Michigan—is indeed telling us not only how *deep* to dig it but *where* to dig it.

Section 5.7.2.d states that, and I'm quoting here: "Earth pit privies shall be located a minimum of one hundred feet (100') from residential and Type IIB non-community and Type III water supplies, and two hundred feet (200') from Type IIA and community water supplies, ten feet (10') from property lines, ten feet (10') from water lines, twenty feet (20') from foundation walls, twenty feet

(20') from building footing drains, storm drains and/or other subsoil drains, twenty-five feet (25') from steep embankments or drop-offs, and seventy-five (75') from lakes, streams or other surface water impoundments. The base of the pit of an Earth Pit Privy shall be a minimum of forty-eight (48") inches above the limiting zone or the seasonal high water table."

A bit more complicated than saying "Eh, Toivo, don't dig it too close to the well." If you've had enough civil-engineering training to follow all that and still dig a legal privy, you probably make enough money to afford indoor plumbing and just forget the whole thing.

Information is still filtering in on the subject. In fact, I'm getting so conversant on potties and privies that perhaps there's an opportunity for a specialty magazine on the latest developments in toilet technology. I'd call it . . . (Are you ready for this?) . . . *Poopular Mechanics*.

ೞ☙

COULD YOU STAND A BIT CLOSER?

The other day I was having coffee with old friends—Blanche Johnson, Ethel Valenzio, Melba Aho, Joan Antilla, and Alice Eman—in the Summer Place Cafe in Republic. I call us old friends because, in fact, we're *OLD*. I checked with the rest of the group before I went public with that statement. Women can be very touchy about age.

We met to make final arrangements for a milestone high-school reunion. Fifty years ago—the spring of 1951—we were among the graduating seniors marching across the frost-warped floor of the Republic High School gymnasium on our way up to the old wooden stage to receive our diplomas. There were twenty-nine of us, the largest Republic graduating class of all time.

In 1951 Harry Truman was president. The first hydrogen bomb was tested in the Pacific. The popular songs were "Shrimp Boats," "They Call the Wind Mariah," and "Getting to Know You." Ben Hogan won the U.S. Open. A new car cost about $1500; a new house, $9000. You could get a gallon of gas for nineteen cents.

We all agreed that name tags—in large print so everyone can read them—would be necessary for the reunion since some folks are coming from far away, and have become—ahem—a bit distinguished-looking over the years.

The people aren't the only thing that's changed over fifty years. The town of Republic has undergone drastic alterations. Not long after we graduated, the Cleveland Cliff Iron Company went into Republic and resurrected the iron mine. As the mine expanded, CCI picked up half of the town buildings and moved them to South Republic. Unfortunately, the old school building couldn't make the trip and was demolished. There's nothing left but a big hole in the ground.

The "girls" and I had a good time going through old photographs. One taken in 1949 was the Republic basketball team. I'm kneeling in the front row with my hand on the basketball. You'd assume I was one of the stars, right? Wrong. The B squad was in the front row because we were the shortest. That was the year I reached the pinnacle of my high-school athletic career. Chet Brown, the high-school principal, suspended four members of the varsity basketball team because one night he caught them smoking cigarettes in the town bowling alley. Coach Alquist had no option but to draft guys from the B squad to fill out the varsity for a road game at National Mine. I saw about five minutes of playing time, got fouled, and made a free throw. It's in the record book.

In 1951 we presented a senior-class play entitled "In Spring The Sap," a three-act farce. In it I played an eighty-nine-year-old inventor. On the night of the play I remember Patricia Flannery, the high-school music teacher, gluing false whiskers on my face followed by a ton of makeup—all to make me look old. Now, I wouldn't need any of that to play the part.

The winter of '50-'51 was super cold with temperatures in the range of -30 to -40 degrees. In March the school had a severe problem with man-size icicles hanging from the eaves. I vividly remember sitting next to the window in the second-floor study hall and flinching whenever the school custodian, standing on the ground below with a 12-gauge shotgun, would fire bird shot up in my direction to knock the icicles down.

All of the high school kids went to Stubby's. Stubby ran the town pool hall, and on Saturday nights he'd open up a makeshift dance hall in a spare room on the second floor. We'd put nickels in the jukebox and dance to Frankie Yankovic's "Blue Skirt Waltz," which got played over and over because it was slow enough for the boys to dance to. The girls danced with each other to Les Paul and Mary Ford, Les playing his amazing, newfangled electric guitar.

One quirky incident in my senior year had a profound effect on the rest of my life. I had spent many hours filling out registration forms for the College of Engineering at the University of Michigan. Then one day one of the high-school teachers told me that my choice was okay, but there just wasn't much demand for engineers. This couldn't have been further from the truth. So I changed my mind and filled out another complete set of applications, this time for the College of Architecture and Design. These later applications must have gotten lost in the U of M admissions office, because the next letter I received informed me that I'd been accepted into the College of Engineering. At age eighteen I had the attention span of a gnat and had grown tired of writing letters and filling out forms. I just let it go. As it turned out, engineering was a good career choice, but I've often wondered what kind of architect I would have made.

It'll really be great to get together with my old classmates again. We can swap stories about ex-spouses, Medicare, Social Security, and the various operations that we've survived. I'm glad there won't be any dancing to the old songs, though. Even in my teenage prime I couldn't keep up with Frankie Yankovic.

₧›₨

FLY-SWATTER SEASON

Summer is here.

And so are the bugs.

Megasquadrons of bloodthirsty mosquitoes—the Michigan state bird—darken the skies, searching for small animals to carry off into the swamp. A few weeks ago I was working at an outdoor festival in Minnesota, and a horde of army worms were munching on a carton of my books. (Maybe they were bookworms, I dunno.) And then there's those microscopic little devil gnats, the no-see-ums, who have a particular need to explore all accessible bodily orifices—mouth, eyes, ears, and nostrils. They're the primary reason that nudist colonies aren't popular in the U.P.

When I was a kid, before the days of universal indoor plumbing and garbage disposals, there were even more bugs around. The flies were particularly bad, lurking around the screen door, just waiting for someone to open it. Kids grew up thinking their name was "Shut the door!"

We had an outhouse in Republic. During the summer, you didn't spend much time relaxing in the privy, reading the Sears catalog, because with the monster blue flies buzzing around you ran the risk of being bitten on extremely private areas.

Back then everyone used flypaper. It came in a small cardboard cylinder that you opened up to pull out a yard of very sticky paper, which was very attractive to flies. In no time at all the flypaper was covered. If you could afford it, you'd hang one in every room in the house, usually from the ceiling light fixtures. When company was invited over, the lady of the house would put up fresh flypaper in their honor. Although they certainly never advertised it, some folks pulled old fly corpses off the flypaper to make it last longer.

Count your blessings that we're too far north for cockroaches. I had plenty of experience with them in California, where the weather is mild year round. One time I found a particularly ugly specimen of cockroach in my Marina del Rey apartment. A large one—about two inches long—that clanked when he walked. I killed it and brought it down to show the apartment-complex manager.

"That's a palmetto bug," she said.

"It looks like a cockroach to me," I replied.

"Yeah, well, it's a palmetto bug."

This is a typical Californian ploy—renaming something disgusting to dress it up with respectability. Palmetto bug almost sounds exotic, doesn't it? Something you'd want to keep around to show off to your friends. They also rename real estate they're trying to sell.

Summertime is also the season for the good bugs. In the early '40's my mother had a big flower garden at our house in Ishpeming. The garden attracted swarms of bumblebees. When the bees were in the hollyhocks, gathering nectar, my friend Jeff and I would sneak up and place an open mason jar up against the flower. When the bee tried to leave he would fly into the jar, and we'd slap the lid on real quick. We weren't totally heartless, though, because the lid had air holes.

The bee in the jar got mad as hell, and it occurred to Jeff and me that if we got *two* bees in the jar, they would probably fight, providing great spectator sport. Employing a tricky transfer involving two jars, we managed to get two bees in a jar, but they weren't as interested in battling each other as they were in getting out of the jar and taking *US* on. As a matter of fact, after doing the two-bees-in-a-jar maneuver a few times, one of the bees got loose and stung me good on the little finger. Jeff and I immediately retired from the bee-slavery business.

I also remember lightning bugs when I was a kid, glowing and dancing around our yard after dusk. Whatever happened to lightning bugs? I haven't seen one in many years. Is it because I go to bed too early now?

This time of year I start keeping a fly swatter next to my bed. I'm pretty lucky where I live in east Marquette, though. The only insects in any great quantity are the spiders on the ceiling of my porch. They're pretty ugly, but I have a live-and-let-live attitude about spiders. I leave them alone because I know they're eating something that's even less desirable than they are.

No question about it, the U.P. is prime bug country in the summer. But don't think too unkindly of these uninvited visitors. Just remember, when they leave, something else is coming to take their place.

It's called snow.

ಬಡಚ

THE ERA OF THE LUMBERJACK

I was having coffee with long-time resident and author Ben Mukkala the other day. Somehow we got to talking about lumberjacks. Ben did a bit of lumberjacking when he was young, and my father spent some time at it in the 1920's. Ben and I agreed that lumberjacks were an important addition to our rich American culture. When it came to drinking, fighting, and chasing loose women, the lumberjacks could easily hold their own with the American cowboys, but for some reason they never got as much media coverage.

In the late 1800's and early 1900's, long before the invention of the present-day power equipment that cuts, limbs, and stacks trees at astonishing speed, it was done with the muscle and sweat of lumberjacks. These guys lived out the cutting season deep in the woods, bunking at logging camps, working from dawn to dusk, using nothing more sophisticated than double-edge axes and long crosscut saws. On their one day off a week they had to sharpen saws and axes, grease boots, and patch their clothes.

Most of the cutting was done during the winter. In those days the easiest way to move harvested logs through the woods was skidding them along iced trails on sleighs pulled by horses or oxen. The logs were deposited at river banks and during the spring thaw floated downstream.

The living conditions at the logging camps were brutally primitive. So primitive that during World War II, when German and Italian prisoners of war were sent to some of the U.P. camps to cut timber, the camps had to be completely rebuilt because they didn't meet the Geneva-Convention standards for humane treatment.

During the winter cutting season, loggers were crammed into log bunkhouses with beds tucked in so close together that they were called "muzzle loaders" because the only way to get in and out of them was at the head or foot. If a bunkhouse had double beds, a wooden plank called a "snortin' board" was put down the middle of the bed to afford some measure of privacy for the two occupants.

Taking a bath at a logging camp was a rare occurrence. Without hot running water, bathing during the winter was nearly impossible. Besides, many lumberjacks believed that regular exposure to soap and water weakened you. Bunkhouses, therefore, had their fair share of minute wildlife. Loggers were always leery of a new guy in camp because he likely brought new little critters with him that may not have been compatible with the ones they already had.

It was a harsh and dangerous existence. You could get maimed by falling trees, crushed by errant logs rolling off a sleigh, or lose your toes from severe frostbite in the frigid winter temperatures. Nevertheless the jacks took a perverse pride in their risky lifestyle. When Henry Ford went into the lumber business in the U.P. he made sure that the working conditions at his camps were much improved. The lumberjacks at other camps scoffed at Ford, labelling his loggers "lumber ladies," which was always good for a bloody knockdown, drag-out brawl whenever the two groups ran into each other in saloons during the off season.

Better roads and the availability of cars for the working class allowed loggers to begin driving back and forth to the job, and by the late 1940's the large logging camps were pretty much a thing of the past.

There were still lumberjacks living in the woods, though. In Upper Michigan, pulp cutters lived by themselves or in pairs in tar-paper shacks next to where they were cutting. The landowner furnished pork and beans, hardtack, coffee, and Peerless chewing tobacco, and the loggers stayed in the woods, cutting and peeling pulp seven days a week. Usually, once a month the boss would drive out, count the sticks of pulp, pay the cutters, and bring them into town.

During my high school years my mother ran a restaurant in Republic. On those weekends when the pulp cutters got paid we had to batten down the hatches. The loggers would storm into the restaurant on Friday night with fistfuls of money. They'd order hot turkey sandwiches, and pump an endless stream of nickels into our old jukebox. They had to have music. All they'd heard for a month were birds and crickets. Many of them couldn't read or could only read Finn, and I often wound up making the jukebox selections for them. Then they charged off to the bars and we wouldn't see them for two days.

Sunday was a different story. The loggers had been evicted from the bars at 2 AM and had grabbed a few hours sleep in empty lots or on sidewalks around Republic. My father got to the restaurant at six in the morning, and the pulp cutters would be standing at the door, waiting for him to open up so they could get coffee. They were bloodshot-eyed, bloody, and broke. Many of them actually smelled pretty good, though, because they'd been drinking after-shave lotion to tide them over until the bars opened again when they would try to bum one last drink before heading back to the woods.

₧ℂℂ

RELIVING A WEDDING DAY

August, 1957—forty-four years ago this week—I was getting married for the first time. If you're wondering why a long-time confirmed bachelor like myself would want to relive such a sinister event, well, all I can say is that time heals all wounds.

I was a newly minted engineer, fresh off the University of Michigan campus, working at White Sands Missile Range in southern New Mexico and renting a one-bedroom apartment in El Paso, Texas, some sixty miles away. My total net worth consisted of four polyester shirts, two pairs of khaki pants, a 1950 Chevrolet, and a 13-inch black-and-white television set. But my new job was paying me the unheard-of sum of $130 a week; so, what the heck, I was ready to take on the world.

I had met my future bride, Emily, at the U of M, and we'd become very friendly during my last semester. So friendly, in fact, that I wanted her around on a full-time basis. That summer Emily was working in Cleveland, and in a fit of blind love and loneliness I proposed over the telephone. She accepted. We set the date for mid August in El Paso. I began scurrying around, making arrangements, even though it was going to be a very small affair.

Emily was coming down by herself, and neither my parents nor my sister could make it, although my mother had fired off a stern letter telling me at the very least to get married in a Lutheran church. I lined up the church and went over to Juarez, Mexico, across the bridge from El Paso, and got fitted for a tailor-made blue serge suit which cost me all of twenty dollars.

Emily arrived at the El Paso airport two days before the wedding. Waiting at the gate, I was bubbling over with love and passion.

My hot blood quickly simmered down, however, when I saw someone getting off the plane with her.

A man.

Emily had somehow made contact with her long-lost father who then decided to attend the wedding.

The father of the bride was dark-haired and swarthy and looked like he could have easily landed a part in "The Godfather." In no time at all he made it quite clear that his primary reason for being there was to make sure that his daughter was legally wed before taking up housekeeping with me. So I had to find Emily a room down the street from my apartment (remember, this was 1957.) Her father took over my bedroom and I slept on the couch.

While getting into my groom suit on the night of the wedding, I was slipping into a state of premarital shock, but the father of the bride was having no problem with jangled nerves. Earlier that day he'd discovered Juarez and the fact that the Mexicans sell very cheap liquor—one dollar for a fifth of bourbon. He'd brought two bottles back across the border. As I dressed, he was putting away the Mexican bourbon at a very smart clip while passing on marital tips.

"The first thing ya gotta do after you're married is to let her know who's boss," he said. It must have been the booze talking because as it turned out, that was very rotten advice.

The wedding at the Lutheran church went off without a hitch, except that after the ceremony the minister was somewhat taken aback when Emily's father began vigorous pumping his hand saying,

"Pastor, that was the best damn wedding ceremony I ever heard!"

Juarez had some good steak houses, so the father of the bride sprang for the wedding dinner across the border. After a few glasses of celebratory champagne, Emily decided that we needed to have wedding pictures taken right then.

"It's too late now," I said. "We can go to a studio in El Paso tomorrow."

That wasn't good enough for her. "You told me that you could get anything, anytime, in Juarez."

"I wasn't talking about wedding pictures."

After dinner I talked to a Juarez cabbie outside the restaurant. At first he wanted to take us to some of the very hottest spots in town, but I explained to him that we'd just gotten married and needed to have wedding pictures. He finally nodded and told the three of us to get in the cab. After a few blocks we found ourselves on a gravel road without street lights. The cabbie pulled up in front of a darkened adobe building and went up to the door and began pounding on it. The door opened and there was a brief discussion in Spanish. The cabbie came back smiling and told us to follow him.

We were led into a living room with a dirt floor. The man living there—the photographer—was in his nightshirt and from a back room he lugged in the biggest, oldest camera I'd ever seen. It's possible that it was Matthew Brady's camera from the Civil War.

The camera was mounted on a gigantic wooden tripod, and the photographer aimed it at a bare wall that had a huge crack running from floor to ceiling. He motioned to us to stand in front of the wall. We stood there, clutching each other's hand, trying to look blissfully happy while facing the camera. The photographer crouched behind the ancient instrument, put his head underneath a heavy cloth, and ignited the flash powder in a wooden hod. It was as bright as a nuclear blast. We were temporarily blinded but had our wedding picture.

Two days later I went to Juarez and picked up the prints.

Emily was not happy with the pictures. "We look like we're standing in front of a Mexican firing squad! We'll have to get better pictures taken here in El Paso."

"That's what I told you the other night in Juarez!" I snapped.

It wasn't the last argument we ever had during our brief married life, but that's another story.

ഈൽ

I'VE TURNED INTO MY FATHER

Every year, when Father's Day rolls around, I relive memories of my old man. It's actually very easy to do because all I have to do is look in the mirror. I've reached the age where I've turned into my father, with the same habits and physical infirmities.

I remember watching my father get out of his favorite old leather rocker. He'd let out this loud grunt. At the time I wondered why he made that funny noise getting out of the chair. Now I get out of my recliner I let out the same loud grunt, and I don't know why I do it either.

Chronic back problems were also something else we shared. For years I paid good money to several medical experts—chiropractors, sports medicine specialists, and orthopedic physicians—trying to find out what was wrong with my back. Finally, I had lower back surgery which—knock on wood—seems to have improved the condition.

My father wasn't inclined to go to doctors and couldn't afford them anyway. He treated his bad back by himself. The old man would lie on his back on the kitchen floor, pull one leg across his body and wedge it beneath the cast-iron wood stove. Then, with the leg held firmly in place by the stove, he'd twist his body in the opposite direction until his vertebrae popped back into place. It seemed to do the trick. But my father was no lightweight, and one day when he was performing this maneuver, the cast-iron stove began to shudder. My mother got very excited and yelled, "If you think the pain in your back is bad, wait till that stove falls on your chest and burns your shirt off!"

I've inherited another physical quirkiness from the old man, which is—to put it politely—a propensity to generate noxious, lighter-than-air gases shortly after eating. We didn't stand on formality at our house. The old man would casually let one rip without giving it a second thought. My mother would soundly chastise him for it, but at the time I thought it was highly amusing. I'm now occasionally afflicted with the same disorder. These are the times when I'm thankful that I live alone.

When I was a kid we'd all gather around the radio in the living room after supper for our evening entertainment. The family loved Jack Benny, Fibber McGee and Molly, and Fred Allen. But if Gabriel Heater or Walter Winchell were on another station, then that's what we listened to because my father always had to hear the latest news. As a kid, I was exposed to so much news that I could have qualified as a World War II military analyst.

The habit remains with me. I tune in to "Headline News" every half hour to see what's happened in the past thirty minutes.

For some reason my father loved burnt toast. We had a toaster, but the old man never used it. He'd toss slices of bread on top of the kitchen wood stove, and when the bread started to smoke he'd flip the pieces over. The toast was as black and as hard as a hockey puck, but that's the way he liked it. Sometimes he'd give me some of this toast for breakfast, and believe it or not I got hooked on the stuff. To this day I crank my toaster up to full dark, but it still doesn't come out as black and as good as stovetop toast.

Like my father I'm a coffee addict, although maybe it's a Scandinavian habit instead of a father-son trait. But the old man, like all of the Finn men in those days, had a style of drinking coffee that I could never master. He'd first place a cube of sugar inside his lower lip and then pour the boiling-hot coffee from his cup into his saucer, whereupon he'd carefully lift the saucer—keeping it completely horizontal—blow on the coffee, and then inhale it into his mouth through the sugar cube. Try it sometime. It ain't easy.

But the most endearing and memorable quality that my father had was never letting life get the upper hand. I don't think I ever saw him upset. I can still remember the waning days of the Depression when jobs were scarce, and even if you had one, it didn't pay nearly enough. My father maintained his sunny outlook throughout it all. If we ran short of money toward the end of the month, the old man would just grin and say something like, "We'd have plenty of money if there wuzn't so many days in the month."

No one told me to adopt this philosophy of good cheer, but it worked so well for the old man that I've tried my best to follow in his footsteps. There are times, though, when I really have to work at it.

Yep, I've turned into my father, and it ain't a bad thing. In fact, I'm proud of it.

෨෭ඏ

IF I WERE THE BASEBALL COMMISSIONER . . .

N ow that the threat of a baseball strike has passed, the major leagues have returned to business as usual—fleecing money from the fans to pay players' salaries.

And a lot of money it is. The average annual salary of a big league baseball player is now well over two million dollars. That's right, *AVERAGE!*. These big bucks, of course, have to be ponied up by the people who come to the ballpark. If a guy plans to take his wife and the two kids to a game, he'd better tap into his retirement fund. By the time he's paid for parking, programs, souvenir caps for the kids, hot dogs, soda pop, beer, and four seats behind third base, he's shelled out over two hundred dollars.

That kind of money just to see a baseball game is outrageous. Baseball shouldn't be an expensive sport to either play or watch. In fact, the other day my friends Jeff and Lidia and I were sitting over coffee at Peggy Sue's Cafe, and in a fit of caffeine-induced enthusiasm we came up with several excellent suggestions to cut costs and save team owners and fans tons of money. Here's what I'd do if I were the Major League Baseball Commissioner.

Use fewer players. When we were kids, playing in the middle of Second Street in South Ishpeming, fire hydrants and parked cars were the bases. On that narrow street there wasn't *ROOM* for nine players on defense. We used no more than four or five players on a side, and it didn't detract from the game one bit. Alex Rodrigues has a 250-million-dollar, ten-year contract to play shortstop for the Texas Rangers. For that kind of money there's no reason why he couldn't play shortstop *AND* second base at the same time, thus eliminating one infielder. And the game could have two outfielders instead of three. So the defense would have more ball chasing to do; what the heck—why not? Higher scores would make the game more exciting. When we were playing street ball it was common for the first team up to bat to score about twenty-six runs—and then go on to lose the game!

And the big leagues don't need all of those pitchers sitting around in the bullpen. Get rid of them and let the starting pitcher throw the whole nine innings. If he doesn't have his good stuff that day, well that's just too bad. When we were kids the only time our pitcher ever left the game was when his mother called him in the house for supper.

They don't have to have all those coaches either. Most of the time coaches just sit around the dugout, scratching themselves and spitting. Even when they're on the field they don't do enough to earn their keep. The job of the first-base coach is to stand there and tell the runner not to take too big a lead or he'll get picked off. This is *NOT* rocket science. The runner knows that; he doesn't need a highly paid coach to tell him. When the pitcher is wild and begins walking batters, it's the pitching coach's job to go out and try to settle him down. Again, not necessary. The catcher could just as easily go to the mound and tell the pitcher, "Hey, meathead, if you can get the ball over the plate sometime soon, I'll line up some chicks and buy the beer after the game." Just let the team manager do all the coaching. He's supposed to know baseball.

Right now they use up between 100-200 baseballs in a major-league game. They could easily get by with no more than a half dozen. Tell the fans to throw the foul balls back onto the field. They'll understand. Who wants a foul ball for a souvenir anyhow? And when a pitcher throws a ball in the dirt the umpire takes it out of play. What a waste. They should just brush the ball off and put it back in play. If a batter can't hit a ball that's slightly dirty, then he doesn't belong in the major leagues. In fact, with proper care a baseball can last a long time. When the stitching came loose we kids used to tape it back together with electrician's tape. Why not do that in the big leagues? Can you imagine what kind of nasty curve Roger Clemens could throw, using a ball patched up with tape?

The same thing with bats. Now, when there's one little crack in the bat it gets thrown away. Bats are expensive. A little tape wrapped around the crack—like we used to do—would keep the bat serviceable for many more games.

So, those are just a few ideas that could save the baseball teams and thus the fans a lot of money. The next time that Jeff and Lidia and I meet at Peggy Sue's we're planning to take on pro basketball.

෨෭ൠ

CHRISTMAS GOODIES FROM THE PAST

I was recently navigating my way through the aisles of Econo Foods, fending off elbows of early Christmas food shoppers when my attention was drawn to a fruitcake display. A wacky image flitted through my mind:

The year is 4000. Two archaeologists are staring down at a fruitcake that they've unearthed from a pile of rubble somewhere on the North American continent.

First Archaeologist: "What do you suppose it is? It looks like something to eat."

Second Archaeologist: "It can't be. Our radiocarbon dating indicates that it's almost two thousand years old, and it's still perfectly intact."

One school of thought is that there's really only one fruitcake in existence which for years has been circulating from person to person each Christmas. I dunno, I think there's got to be at least fifty or sixty of them.

Seriously, when I was a kid my mother made fruitcake every Christmas, and it was delicious. Of course, throughout the rest of the year the standard dessert fare on our dinner table was stewed prunes or rhubarb pudding, so I always looked forward to the special sweets at Christmas.

Would you believe that oranges used to be a Christmas treat? During the '30's and '40's many fruits weren't readily available in the U.P. during the winter. But special shipments of oranges made their way up here during the Christmas holidays. Dates were another fruit we saw only at Christmas. Like the oranges they came from the magical kingdom called California where none of us had ever been.

The Finns had their own special Christmas food. I remember kulta velliä (rough translation—gold pudding). The principal ingredients were raisins and dried apricots, and it was very tasty. At Christmas we also had the Finnish cheese (juustoa), popularly known as "squeaky cheese," so named, I think, because it squeaks when you bite into it. Unfortunately, it's still around. I hated it as a kid, and I still hate it. People say to me, "What kind of Finn are you if you don't like squeaky cheese?" I'm the kind of Finn who doesn't like saunas either.

Nuts were another cherished Christmas item—in the shell, of course. My mother would put out a big bowl of walnuts, hazelnuts, almonds, and Brazil nuts, along with the nutcracker. The shells on Brazil nuts were so tough that my father was the only one of us who could crack them. I was fourteen years old before I could break the shells myself.

And my mother always made saffron bread for the holidays. In fact, she did so faithfully until she was almost ninety. Saffron usually comes from Spain, the dried stigma from the crocus flower. Making saffron bread during the Depression must have really pinched the pocketbook because saffron has always been the most expensive spice you can buy. It currently sells for about $40 an ounce, so if you receive some saffron bread this Christmas, eat it very slowly.

My mother also baked prune tarts. Nowadays you see prune tarts all the time, but back then the tarts were special and only made their appearance during Christmas.

The Lutheran church in Ishpeming would pass out boxes of those hard Christmas candies to all of the Sunday School kids after the Christmas Eve service. These were the least favorite of the Christmas candies. They were as dense as rocks and didn't have much taste, but, of course, we ate them anyway.

And who could forget the Christmas animal crackers that came in a colorful little box that looked like one of those old circus wagons? As a small kid I took great delight in drowning the animals in a glass of milk, then fishing them out with a spoon and eating them.

I also remember the Wintergreen mints that came in a long, thin box. I think they were pure sugar with a bit of flavoring added, but who cares? I loved them.

Speaking of sugar, a lot of the Christmas sweets weren't nearly as sweet after sugar rationing kicked in during World War II. The ration allotment was a half pound of sugar per person per week. Up to that time my old man was using twice that much just in his morning coffee. A lot of enterprising but sacrificing folks gave away one pound bags of sugar as Christmas presents. That was one gift that didn't get returned to the store.

∞∞

OLD-TIME RADIO COMMERCIALS

The other evening I was having dinner at the Northwoods Club with my friends, Jeff and Lidia, and somehow we got on the subject of old-time radio commercials. Jeff finished off his glass of wine and suddenly broke into song.

"Pepsi-Cola hits the spot.
Twelve full ounces, that's a lot.
Twice as much for a nickel, too.
Pepsi-Cola is the drink for you."

This really astonished our young waitress, not Jeff's singing so much, but she couldn't believe that Pepsi at one time was only a nickel a bottle. I offered to buy Jeff another glass of wine to see if he would sing any more, but he declined.

Those old radio commercials bring back waves of nostalgia. I remember listening to fifteen-minute episodes of "Jack Armstrong, the All-American Boy," and during the commercial break a barbershop quartet, in close harmony, would belt out:

"Have you tr.....ied Wheaties?
They're whole wheat with all of the bran.
Won't you tr.....y Wheaties?
For wheat is the best food of man.
They're crispy and crunchy the whole year through.

The kiddies will never tire of them, and neither will you.
Won't you tr.....y Wheaties?
The best breakfast food in the land."

One of my favorites was the Postum commercial because it had a plot, complete with a dastardly villain. The bad guy was (play spooky organ music here) Mr. Coffee Nerves, a satanic character who would jab a sharp instrument into the central nervous system of a coffee-drinking housewife and then laugh fiendishly when the jittery woman began yelling at her innocent children. Invariably, the distraught heroine would kick the coffee habit when she discovered caffeine-free Postum, and Mr. Coffee Nerves would slink back into the darkness, muttering, "Curses, foiled again by Postum!"

And who could forget Johnny, the little bellboy who advertised Phillip Morris cigarettes by shouting out:

"CALL FOR PHILLIP MORRIS!
CALL FOR PHILLIP MORRIS!"

Johnny actually was a bellhop working at the New Yorker Hotel when a Phillip Morris advertising executive gave him a dollar to page Phillip Morris in the lobby. Johnny did such a good job at it that he received a lifetime contract, appearing on many radio and early TV shows.

How about this one?

"You'll wonder where the yellow went
when you brush your teeth with Pepsodent."

And the Bromo-Seltzer's talking train with the steam-whistle voice:

"FFFFiiiigggghhhhttttt headache three ways!
BromoSeltzer BromoSeltzer BromoSeltzer BromoSeltzer...."

Or: "Halo everybody Halo.
Halo is the shampoo that glorifies your hair.
So Halo everybody Halo.
Halo Shampoo Halo!"

How many of you remember the stern announcer blaring out:
"The FBI in Peace and War!
Brought to you by Lava Soap!
L-A-V-A! L-A-V-A!"
And don't forget that "Lifebuoy really stops (fog-horn sound)
Beeee-Ohhhh!!!!"

If you thought that Little Orphan Annie was merely an unfortunate waif, constantly harassed by a host of evil scoundrels, you're wrong. On the side, Annie was an enterprising marketeer, hawking her brightly colored shake-up mug that you had to have in order to mix and drink your delicious, chocolaty, energy-fortified Ovaltine. She also pushed other essentials like her famous decoder ring. I swallowed a lot of Ovaltine taking directions from Little Orphan Annie.

World War II had some memorable radio commercials. Before the war, the Lucky Strike cigarette package was green with a red circle in the center. But in 1942 the green dye was needed for uniforms, tanks, cannons, etc, so the Lucky Strike people redesigned the package—white with the red circle, as it is today. The tobacco company saw the opportunity for some great advertising, and they employed a drill-sergeant announcer to bark out:
"Lucky Strike green has gone to war! (bass drum beat)
Yes, Lucky Strike green *HAS* gone to war!"

I imagine that there were people who took up cigarette smoking after hearing that patriotic message.

And finally there was another WWII commercial. This is from Arrid.
"Is the sweetheart you married the husband you expected?
Is the war creating new problems in your marriage?"

The pitch implied that the war was creating new pressures that produced excessive underarm perspiration, severely straining marriages and friendships. In other words, Is the war making you nervous? Better try Arrid.

That old commercial makes sense even today, doesn't it? George W. Bush and Saddam Hussein are going toe to toe. The North Koreans are firing missiles. Iran is getting plutonium from Russia. We don't know what Osama bin Laden is up to. Maybe we should all go out and get some Arrid.

ഇൻൽ

YEARS OF LIVING DANGEROUSLY

D o you senior citizens ever wonder how you survived childhood? I know I do.

I was born at home in a somewhat less-than-sterile environment. Dr. McCann made a house call to South Ishpeming to bring me into this world. Up to the last minute even that decision was a subject of lively debate between my mother and her friends. Most of the neighborhood women had given birth to many children and were perfectly capable and willing to midwife the event. My parents could have saved the twenty-dollar doctor's fee.

There was no protective padding on my crib, and the bars were wide enough so I could easily stick my head between them to observe the outside world. Sudden Infant Death Syndrome hadn't been invented yet. When I went to sleep at night I was on my own.

When I was still a toddler, my mother would put me on the living-room floor and scatter out a large quantity of shirt buttons on the carpet. I would play with them for hours. How many did I swallow? Who knows? However, everything seemed to work out okay.

There were no child-safety seats nor, for that matter, seat belts of any type in automobiles. Children rattled around in the back seat, unencumbered.

We played baseball in the middle of Second Street in Ishpeming, having to frequently halt the game to let cars drive through our infield. There were no batting helmets or protective cups, and a catcher's mask was something we'd only heard about. In fact, barely half of us owned gloves, and this was baseball, not softball; the pitcher threw overhand. We had plenty of banged-up fingers, scrapes, and gashes, some of them from running into third base, which happened to be a fire hydrant.

When we weren't playing baseball we were racing up and down the Ishpeming alleys, dodging old boards full of rusty nails, jagged pieces of tin, and broken bottles. We dug around in maggot-infested garbage cans, hunting for valuables that we could bring home.

My friend Jeff and I lived next to the LS&I railroad tracks where there was a plentiful supply of chunks of iron ore dropped from the passing ore trains. A favorite sport was getting into pitched battles with the Catholic kids where we pegged iron ore at each other. One time I got hit so hard on the head that it filled up my cap with blood. My mother washed out the wound and swabbed some iodine on it. That was it. No doctor's visit.

On Halloween we put on our costumes and charged out into the dark streets to go trick or treating. There were no adults along to watch us go up to each door because the grownups were all at home protecting their own property. This was *REAL* trick or treating, and all of us carried a bar of wax to use on the windows of stubborn home owners who didn't come across with candy. We began stuffing the candy into our mouths on the way home. There were no parental post-Halloween candy inspections, looking for hidden razor blades.

In the winter Jeff and I used to ski jump on a small hill next to our houses. We wore no protective gear, unless you wanted to count our long underwear.

There were no crossing guards at the intersections along the route when I walked to school. In fact, being at school was more dangerous than getting there, because the teachers wouldn't hesitate to belt you a good one for any minor infraction.

As a teenager in Republic I ran my own trap line in the winter. Every day after school, even during snowstorms, I put on my skis and took off into the woods to check the traps. For proprietary reasons I naturally didn't tell anyone where this trap line ran, not even my parents. If I had fallen and broken a leg, I wouldn't have been found till the spring thaw.

Kids aren't exposed to that kind of environment nowadays, and of course in many ways that's good. Today's children are protected from birth through high school; they're sanitized, medicated, vaccinated, harnessed, helmeted, padded, and shielded from maniacs by watchful adults.

But are these kids really better off? I'm not sure. The news is full of frightening statistics about obesity in children reaching epidemic proportions. Many are being diagnosed with diabetes; some will even have heart disease before they're teenagers. Why? Because they're vegging out in front of TV's and computers, all the while gulping down King-Kong-size helpings of French fries and potato chips. We kids used to eat a lot of fattening foods, too, but, of course, that was before cholesterol was invented. Seriously, we'd go outside and run it off. My suggestion is to have parents pull the plugs on the TV and computer, yank the kids off the couch, and push their fat fannies out the door to go and play. It'll do them good. Tell them not to come home until dark.

☙❧

70 YEARS OF CHANGES

O n April 16 I turned seventy. I woke up that morning and said to myself, "Hey, seventy isn't so old. Now, eighty, *THAT'S* old." (Of course, I said the same thing about seventy when I turned sixty.) My appetite is good, and there's still a definite spring in my step as I head for my recliner. And my appearance is still youthful if you squint at me from a distance in subdued light.

But I know I've been around the block a few times when I realize how many now-commonplace things have been introduced in my lifetime.

In this modern age, everything is made of plastic. You can't get away from it. When I was a small kid there was no plastic. (Can you imagine a world without shrink-wrap?) All we had was paper, wood, glass, and metal. When you bought a shirt at J.C. Penny's in downtown Ishpeming, the clerk wrapped it up in brown paper and tied the package with white string. (There was no Scotch tape either.) Milk came in glass bottles. I used to save my pennies to buy toy cars, all made of cast iron. In my backyard, sand-box disputes were often settled by flinging an iron toy truck at your adversary, truly an assault with a deadly weapon.

Today's teenagers buy their music on CD's. My first introduction to recorded music was a 78 rpm record played on an old Victrola that you had to crank. I was already in high school when 45 and 33-1/3 rpm records came out to replace the 78's. People were outraged because they had to go out and buy a three-speed record player that used two different phonograph needles. I actually thought it was a pretty neat thing, though, because you could play a 45 rpm record of the Sons of the Pioneers singing "Cool Water" at 78 rpm, and they came out sounding like the Three Chipmunks.

Speaking of music, I remember listening to Les Paul and Mary Ford doing "How High the Moon" on one of the first multi-track recordings. People had never heard an electric guitar before, much less two of them played simultaneously by the same person backing up a woman who was singing a duet with herself.

Nowadays, with meteorological satellites and sophisticated computer software, one can be reasonably sure what to expect weatherwise for the next several days. In the '30's and '40's, before computers were around and the moon was the only satellite orbiting the earth, severe weather was pretty much a nasty surprise. One of the most popular weather-forecasting aids was lumbago. My old man could tell us whenever a blizzard was due just from the ache in his hip. A lot of people did this sort of folksy bone forecasting, but some were better at it than others, and the good ones acquired quite a reputation. People would go and visit their neighbor Jalmer to see how he was feeling, not because they really cared about his welfare, but they wanted to know what to expect for weather the next day.

I remember when homogenized milk first made the scene. Before that, the milkman deposited the milk in bottles on the front porch with about three inches of cream in the top layer. The first time we got homogenized milk my mother asked the milkman where the cream was. He explained that it was all mixed together now.

"What am I going to put in my coffee?" she wanted to know.

"Well, you buy the cream separately now," he replied.

My mother thought that homogenized milk was a pretty stupid idea and held that belief until the day she died in 1997.

I also remember when technicolor movies first came out. People flocked to the theater, not to see their favorite actor or actress, but because it was in color. The first technicolor movie I saw was the 1941 version of *Billy the Kid* with Robert Taylor. I sat through two showings at the Ishpeming Theater and came home with a splitting headache. My mother didn't want me to go to any more technicolor movies because they were too hard on the eyes.

How many of you remember 1949, the year of the radical design change in automobiles? They came out without fenders. I went down to Hooper's Garage in Republic to gawk at the new 1949 Ford in the showroom. Some guys said that these cars would never catch on because without fenders there was no way to get your buck out of the woods during deer season.

In 1961, between wives, I discovered the newly marketed TV dinners. For a couple of years my week's grocery shopping consisted of two six packs of beer and a stack of Swanson TV dinners. After I met Joanne, my second wife, I quit eating those things and haven't turned on an oven since.

Well, that's not exactly true. I do use a microwave oven. I can remember back around 1970 when microwaves first became popular. Store demonstrators, usually women, would heat food in the microwave and pass it around for customers to sample. Many people wouldn't touch the food because they were afraid it was radioactive. The demonstrator had to calm their fears by eating a heated sample herself to prove that she wasn't going to glow in the dark.

I was twenty-four years old when I bought my first TV, a 13-inch black and white. In 1965 Joanne and I bought a color set, and we spent every evening camped in front of it. I would have been a pioneer couch potato except that I had to get up every five minutes to adjust the color or change channels. It didn't come with a remote control.

I don't know how many more of these scientific breakthroughs I'll see in my remaining years. I just wish that someone could repeal the law of gravity so my chest would go back up to where it was when I was twenty.

ৼয়ৢঽ

A MOTOR-HOME TALE

Summer is the season when everyone hits the road and goes camping. For many, however, modern-day camping is a far cry from heating pork and beans over an open fire and curling up in a sleeping bag beneath the stars. Nowadays a lot of people buy a motor home. Most of these behemoths—price tags well into six figures—have expandable living rooms, large-screen TV's, microwave ovens, dishwashers, king-size beds, and Jacuzzis. This is camping?

I once owned a motor home. A DeSoto. Never heard of a DeSoto motor home, you say? Well, I had one.

In 1958 I was newly married and working as a junior engineer at Douglas Aircraft in Santa Monica, California. My bride, Emily, was a student at UCLA with zero income. In those days we were so financially strapped that when the wolf came to our door we ate it.

But every weekend we'd strike out from our tiny apartment in search of adventure because our hearts were young and gay. (This was back in the days when gay had a different meaning.)

That summer we bought a 1947 DeSoto for $250. The car had an asthmatic engine, bald tires, and Chrysler's early experimental version of fluid drive which took about a minute or so after you pressed the gas pedal to realize that you wanted to go forward.

But the DeSoto had one very attractive feature. Room. It was an old limousine with a pair of jump seats in the rear. When the seats were folded up you could easily sleep two across on the rear floor. This was our motor home.

One weekend we decided to explore Mexicali, a Mexican border town out in the desert across from the city of Calexico on the California side. We loaded up the DeSoto with pillows, blankets (sleeping bags weren't in our budget), groceries, and beer. The plan was to explore Mexico and then come back to Calexico, find a nice secluded town park, and camp for the night in our cozy motor home.

That was the plan.

Everything was going just swell until about midnight when we began looking for a campsite. There weren't any parks in Calexico—only dark, dusty streets with suspicious characters skulking along the sidewalks. We proceeded out of town and wound up on an unpaved road. There were no trees, only sand and sagebrush and a bad smell that we couldn't identify. I decided to turn around, but the road was too narrow, so I drove on, searching for a wide spot. We finally came up on an expanse of hardpan. The smell was getting worse.

I backed the DeSoto out onto the hardpan to turn around. But when I got all four wheels onto it, the heavy limo broke through a sun-baked two-inch crust. We sunk into what turned out to be the entire sewage output from the city of Calexico. Our motor home was up to the axles in a sea of poop.

I put the DeSoto in forward, then reverse, trying to rock loose, but the wheels just went ZZZZZZZ, sending up a thick spray of you-know-what.

Every flying insect in the state of California and all the northern provinces of Mexico smelled the result and zeroed in on us. My wife began moaning piteously.

I had no shovel, but there was a small metal panel in the trunk which had fallen off from somewhere on the car, so I began using it in a futile attempt to dig us out. The bugs went insane with glee. Emily was sitting in the limo, loudly questioning the wisdom of agreeing to be my spouse.

By and by, headlights appeared along the road. A Border Patrol officer in a jeep pulled up and shined a flashlight on us, thinking that we were illegals crossing over from Mexico.

When he saw our blonde heads he asked, "What in the world are you people doing out here? Do you know what this is?"

We explained our situation and that, yes, we now had a pretty good idea what it was that we were in. He had a good laugh over that and then told us that he'd pull us out. He got in his jeep and began backing out onto the hardpan to attach a cable to the front of the DeSoto.

"Don't drive onto it," I cried. "You'll break through like we did!"

He turned and looked at me, laughing heartily. "Don't worry. I've got four-wheel drive."

His jeep did, in fact, break through the crust, but the officer wasn't troubled at all. He attached a steel cable to the front of the DeSoto. We both got into our vehicles, put them in gear, and stomped on the gas pedals.

Six wheels going ZZZZZZ can churn up a lot more poop than two wheels. The four-wheel-drive jeep dug itself in even deeper than the DeSoto. Being behind the jeep, my windshield instantly turned dark brown, along with the hood, grill and front fenders. The bugs were now inviting their relatives in from Nevada, Arizona, and New Mexico. Emily's moaning had now turned into a shrill screech.

The Border Patrol officer no longer saw any humor in the situation. In fact, he became downright grumpy. He got on his two-way radio and began barking at someone at the Border Patrol headquarters. Soon another jeep appeared.

"Don't drive out on this stuff!" the first officer yelled at the new arrival.

With the second jeep remaining on the road, we hooked up the three vehicles in tandem and churned away. Slowly but surely, through a brown blizzard, my DeSoto motor home rose out of the poop lagoon. It was not a pretty sight.

The two officers told us to get out of there and never darken their border again. In the early morning light we took off for Los Angeles. The limo was filthy and the smell was horrific. Palm trees wilted along the highway as we passed. It was hard to navigate because the wipers were glued to the windshield.

That was my first and last motor home. I sold the DeSoto soon afterward. I don't remember who bought it, but as I recall, I had the buyer standing upwind of the vehicle until the deal was closed.

৯৩৫

MEMORIES OF NOT SHOOTING STRAIGHT

The other day I was having lunch at Peggy Sue's Cafe with my friends Lidia and Jeff. Lidia had been taking a riflery class and showed us one of her targets. At fifty feet, using a .22-caliber target rifle, she'd put a five-shot cluster in the bull's-eye that could've been covered with a quarter. Both Jeff and I had to admit that this was a fine piece of shooting.

I could never shoot straight. Of course, as a kid I was deadly accurate when pointing my finger and going "BANG! BANG!" And with a cap pistol I was better than Hopalong Cassidy. But when I graduated to something that actually fired a projectile it was a different story. Maybe it was the habit of closing my eyes and flinching before I even put my finger on the trigger.

At age thirteen I got a BB gun—a Daisy 50-shot pump-action repeater. I eagerly loaded the gun and took it out to the Republic dump where I filled the air with BB's, shooting at the rats. No luck. Day after day I went out there and futilely blasted away. After awhile the rats thought it was some kind of game, and they'd laugh and squeal and form a chorus line right in front of my gun sight.

A few years later I got my first real firearm, a single-shot .22 rifle. I went rabbit hunting that winter, but the bunnies had nothing to fear. I didn't have any better luck than I did with the rats in the dump.

When I turned sixteen I was old enough to get a hunting license, and that fall I was determined to go partridge hunting. My father made it clear that he wasn't going to finance a shotgun, so I had to begin saving my nickels and quarters.

From the 1949 Sears catalog I ordered the cheapest shotgun they had—a seven-dollar 20-gauge single-shot with a hollow plastic stock. Don't laugh, it'd be a collector's item today.

My old man couldn't believe it when I opened the Sears package and showed him the shotgun. He'd heard about plastic—the innovative new material—but a plastic gun stock?

We took the Sears shotgun out in the woods to try it out. Because the hollow plastic stock was so light, the gun kicked like a crazed mule when you fired it. We brought it back home, and the old man took off the stock's butt plate and crammed in an assortment of old nuts and bolts that were lying around our woodshed. With the added weight the gun didn't recoil near so much, but it now rattled when you carried it.

Partridges were even more difficult to hit than rabbits or rats because they could fly. I did manage to get one partridge that season—a close-up ground shot. The bird was hypnotized by the rattling shotgun.

Not only couldn't I shoot straight, but I wasn't familiar with the laws of physics, either. That fall when flocks of geese flew over, heading south, I'd stand in the backyard with my 20-gauge and blast away at them. The geese didn't even break formation. My father tried to explain that the geese were flying well above the range of my shotgun, but I couldn't resist the temptation and kept shooting at them anyway. The old man just stood on the back porch, shaking his head. I think he figured that when it came to hunting savvy I took after my mother.

In November I joined the big-league hunters and got my first deer license. The old man willed me his rifle. This rifle had been lying in a closet for about 25 years and was *REALLY* a collector's piece—a .32 Remington pump action that dated back to at least 1910. It had a long, hexagonal barrel and weighed about 190 pounds. It fired a rimless cartridge that no one carried anymore.

I finally laid my hands on a box of cartridges at an exorbitant price and then shot up half of them trying to sight in the rifle. It didn't make any difference because I didn't get off a shot all that season. I made the near-fatal error of hunting east of Republic where a large number of down-state appleknockers had their deer camps. After some of these guys had a few beers under their belts they weren't terribly fussy about what they took a shot at. There were more flying bullets than deer out there.

I spent the next deer season in the Republic cemetary hiding behind a pile of rocks, trying to ambush a large buck that crossed through there early every morning. The buck was considerably smarter than me. He'd either cross the cemetery before I got there in the morning or wait until I took a midmorning coffee break at my grandmother's house nearby. All I got that season was frostbite.

In the 1960's I did some hunting in California. Ed and Jo Ann Weaver, a couple that my wife (second ex-wife, Joanne) and I knew, were seasoned hunters and introduced us to chukkar hunting. The chukkar is a desert game bird that flies so fast it makes the cartoon Roadrunner look like the Goodyear blimp. I blew up a lot of sagebrush but never hit a single chukkar.

On one of those trips Ed was doing some target shooting with his .357 Magnum revolver. The .357 is a huge handgun that fires a slug big enough to bring down a charging rhinoceros.

Ed handed me the .357 and pointed at a tin can about fifty feet away. "Try your luck," he said.

At last, I thought, something that's not running or flying. I took careful aim at the can and pulled the trigger.

The next thing I knew I was stone deaf. The smoking revolver barrel was pointing straight up but waving around because my right hand was totally numb. My boots had plowed six-foot furrows backwards in the sand from the recoil.

"Did I hit the can?" I asked Ed.

"You didn't even hit the ground," he said. "I think the slug is in orbit."

"Let me try that," my wife said. Joanne was only five-foot two with small hands.

"Better not," I warned. "You'll hurt yourself."

But she took the heavy revolver with both hands, cocked the hammer using two thumbs, aimed at the can, and fired.

She drilled the can dead center.

Realizing that everyone on the planet is a better shot than I am, I haven't fired a gun in a long time. But when the leaves begin changing color in the crisp fall air, my thoughts always turn to hunting. I somehow resist the urge. However, if you should see me out in the woods with some kind of firearm in my hands, you'd best exercise caution. Stand in my line of fire; that would be the safest place.

ട്ടാരു

WHEN DOGS WERE JUST DOGS

My cousin Karen, in Texas, is a doting parent of two dogs. The other day she FAX'd me an article from the *Houston Chronicle* which describes just how far modern-day dog owners have gone to pamper their pets.

If you're in the market for a pure-bred dog—with papers, of course—be prepared to shell out upwards of three thousand dollars. And that's just for openers. According to the article, if you want to take proper care of your new pet, you'll need an orthopedic doggie bed, equipped with electric heating or cooling units and also a recirculating water bowl to keep his drinking water from becoming stagnant. Because your dog will want to go everywhere with you, another must-have accessory is a canine car-safety seat.

Dog owners are now spending billions of dollars annually on their four-footed "children." Today's pooches have faux leopard-skin leashes, squeaky toys that look like cats, fur-lined jackets and booties for cold weather, rhinestone-studded collars, mother-of-pearl-inlaid pooper scoopers, toothbrushes, and (Are you ready for this?) beef-flavored toothpaste.

Groomers get big bucks for bathing your dog with scented soap, cleaning ears, clipping toenails, and trimming and shaping your pet's coat. Dogs make regular visits to their veterinarian, not just for the required shots, but also treatment for intestinal parasites, eye and ear infections, skin problems, arthritis, and even canine Alzheimers. If you live in California—I'm not making this up—you can find a doggie psychiatrist if your pet has trouble dealing with the stresses of modern canine life. There is a celebrated pet psychic in Houston who claims she is able to talk to your poochie to discuss physical and mental health problems.

When I was a kid, dogs were just dogs. Nobody ever bought a dog; they were free. There was no such thing as pet neutering, so there was always a plentiful pooch supply. When someone's lady dog had a litter of pups, the owner couldn't give them away fast enough. No one had leashes, so there were all kinds of dogs roaming the streets of Ishpeming. Some dogs didn't even have owners; they were hobo dogs that dug around in alley garbage cans, doing the best they could.

None of these dogs were purebred; we didn't even know what purebred meant. When I saw *Lassie Come Home* at the Butler Theater in Ishpeming I thought to myself, "What a great-looking dog." I'd never seen a purebred collie before.

All dogs had fleas because they spent most of their life outside, and there were no flea collars. Only in the dead of winter, when the fleas had packed up and gone south, were dogs allowed to spend the night indoors.

I had a dog; his name was Teddy. Teddy was a mutt, though someone said that he was part Spitz. I got him as a puppy, and one of our neighbors—a good carpenter—built Teddy a little doghouse. Teddy loved it and slept in it every night. But at age eight I was deep into my carpentry period and decided that the doghouse was much too small. Nailing together a bunch of discarded fruit crates from the A&P, I constructed a beautiful, but slightly ramshackle, multi-room, two-story "dog hotel." It had a neat ramp to get to the second floor. I showed Teddy my creation and even pushed him up the ramp so he could check out the upper-story rooms. He took one look around the dog hotel and began whimpering, then ran down the ramp, and crawled into his little doghouse. Teddy was a good dog, though, except for his lack of taste of the finer things in life.

Dog food was a luxury that most folks couldn't afford. Dogs ate leftovers—old hash, cold string beans, bread crusts, dried oatmeal, anything that came off the table that no one wanted. If the dog didn't like it, that was just too bad. He could always check out what was available in the alleys.

Back in those days there were lumberjacks and pulp cutters living in tar-paper shacks in the woods, and these guys didn't feed their dogs at all. The dogs existed on whatever they could run down in the woods. Afterward, generations of dogs were running deer in the U.P. because by then it was genetic.

Dogs also inherited a strong urge to chase cars, dating back to the days when there weren't many cars around. One gutsy pooch in South Ishpeming—a hobo dog we called Brownie—set his sights much higher and took up chasing the ore trains that rumbled by our house. Unfortunately, he caught one, and afterward we called him Three Legs. Although he survived, Three Legs had to give up chasing ore trains and cars because with one leg missing he'd slowed down considerably.

So, it was a tough life for dogs back in those days. They had a short life expectancy. No balanced diet or shots. If a dog got sick, he either got well or he didn't because no one took him to a vet. Or he could have gotten seriously maimed or even killed in the frequent dogfights that broke out in the streets and alleys.

But the survivors were tough. They were unleashed, could potty anytime and anywhere they pleased, and had a love life that wasn't curtailed by surgical procedures. These pups were free and footloose. They certainly wouldn't have had any use for a canine psychiatrist.

DOING HARD TIME

Over lunch at Peggy Sue's Cafe the other day, my friend Jeff and I were discussing our mutual experiences in jail. It's true. We've both served jail time.

Jeff began his criminal career at a very early age. One hot summer night when he was eleven (after I'd moved away from Ishpeming) Jeff and a few buddies discovered a freight car filled with watermelons sitting on a siding in downtown Ishpeming. The freight car was locked tight, but the wooden slats on the sides were wide enough apart to clearly see the watermelons. In fact, wide enough to insert a long-bladed kitchen knife between the slats and cut slices from one of the melons, which is precisely what Jeff did. He was busily hacking pieces from a watermelon next to the slats and passing them back to his eager pals when a flashlight lit up the crime scene.

A cop grabbed Jeff by the collar and hauled him down to the police station on Division Street. His father was summoned and soon appeared at the station to hear the watermelon-larceny charges against his son.

Jeff's old man, a tough iron miner, was a strong advocate of stern justice. "Lock 'im up!" he told the desk sergeant.

And that's exactly what happened. Eleven-year-old Jeff was

locked in a cell all by himself where he spent the night picturing a grim future decked out in a striped suit and breaking up large rocks with a sledgehammer.

The next morning Jeff's father returned to the station. A mock trial was held with the desk sergeant presiding, and Jeff was released on "parole" in his father's custody. The jail time worked. Jeff hasn't stolen a thing in sixty years.

Now, my story. In 1976 I was forty-three, living in Marina del Rey, California, frantically trying to ward off impending middle age with garish hippy clothing, folk singing, sailboating, and beer parties. One Saturday afternoon I was on a friend's sailboat in Long Beach harbor. Sailing and beer drinking go hand in hand, and in the course of four or five hours I put away several brews. After we docked I drove toward home, drowsy from the sun and beer. I got back to Marina del Rey and stopped at my favorite restaurant for a fish dinner. Unfortunately, I elected to wash the meal down with two glasses of wine which destroyed any remaining vestiges of sobriety. I took off for home, now driving *VERY* slowly.

The one thing you should never do in California is drive slow. If you're going less than seventy miles an hour—even in your driveway—it arouses suspicion. As I approached my apartment, I noticed flashing red lights in the rear view mirror. I pulled over to the curb, and the cop politely instructed me to get out of the vehicle. He then put me through a battery of tests involving touching my nose (I poked my eye instead) and walking the straight crack in the sidewalk. The next thing I knew I was in handcuffs in the back of a patrol car with no inside door handles, heading for the West Los Angeles Police Precinct.

You can really sober up in a hurry when a cop jams your fingers onto an ink pad, takes your fingerprints, and then stands you up against a white wall with height markings for a frontal and profile shot. I had to empty all of my pockets, and my possessions were scooped into a large paper bag. This included my shoelaces.

A uniformed deputy put me into a large room, no windows except for the one in the thick steel door. The only furniture was a seatless toilet in the corner. The walls and floor were coated with rubberized foam to keep the occupants from hurting themselves. It was your classic rubber-room drunk tank.

At the time there was only one other guy in the room. He rushed up to me with a cigarette in his hand.

"You gotta match?" he asked with urgency.

As luck would have it, a book of matches in my shirt pocket had been overlooked. I gave him the matches, and he hurriedly lit up the cigarette.

Except that it wasn't a cigarette. Really desperate for a smoke, the bozo had tightly rolled up some toilet paper from the corner potty. A split second after lighting up the "cigarette," he took a quick drag before it went up in a ball of flame and smoke. The deputy, glancing through the door window, saw the smoke, barged in, and grabbed the matches.

As the evening wore on, the room filled up rapidly. There is no reality show on TV that can remotely compare to a Los Angeles drunk tank on a Saturday night. Try to imagine all of the undesirables from every movie you've ever seen—tough guys, con men, braggarts, drifters, thieves, religious zealots, garden-variety bums—and you'd have a pretty good idea of my cellmates that night. And every last one was snockered to the gills. The room rocked with screams, curses, singing, threats, fights, and preaching. I finally laid down on the rubber floor in a corner and shut my eyes. But I bolted upright every time one of my "roommates" patted me down to see if I had anything of value, which, of course, I didn't.

Fortunately, I'd used my one telephone call to contact my girlfriend. At 2AM (the police wouldn't let me go until the bars closed) she arrived and I was released in her custody.

I wound up paying a hefty fine and shortly thereafter gave up drinking entirely.

Then, in 1996 I moved back to the U.P. During my first physical exam in Marquette the doctor asked me, "Mr. Harju, do you drink?"

"No, sir," I answered proudly.

He smiled. "Well, a daily glass or two of wine can actually be beneficial for a man your age."

And who says that God doesn't have a sense of humor?

୨୦ଔ

THE OLD MAN AND THE SEA(WEED)

For a long time I thought fishing was all a matter of luck. As a kid in the U.P. I tied fishing line to the end of a long stick, fastened a hook and sinker to the line, added a worm, and tossed it in the water. What could be simpler? The rest was up to the fish. If I didn't catch anything, well, the fish just weren't biting that day. Just a matter of luck.

Then, in 1968 my wife Joanne, stepson Greg, our dog Thunderball, and I took a summer camping trip up the West Coast. At age thirteen, Greg was crazy about fishing (two years later girls had replaced fish). Driving north from Los Angeles we dipped our lines into several promising lakes but didn't catch a thing. Just bad luck, I told Greg. However, I'd heard that the Rogue River in Oregon had salmon the size of railroad ties, and that's where we headed. Sure enough, on a solitary beach on the Rogue we found the bones and heads of large salmon in the sand where lucky fishermen had feasted on the huge fish. Greg got very excited. So did Thunderball who gleefully rolled around in the fish heads.

Just as we got our tent put up, a logging truck stopped on a nearby bridge that spanned the river. The driver got out with a fishing pole and dropped his line into the fast-moving water. Within minutes he pulled out an enormous salmon. Greg and I rushed up to the bridge just as the trucker was placing the salmon into a large cooler.

"What did you use to catch that fish?" I asked eagerly.

He showed us a red-and-white striped spoon lure called a Daredevil. Naturally, we didn't have any in our meager tackle box.

"You can get these at that little store four miles down the road," the trucker said.

Greg and I jumped in my pickup and raced down the winding dirt road to the store. We bought three Daredevils—one extra, just in case—and sped back to the campsite to catch our salmon.

It took us less than ten minutes to lose all three lures to snags in the fast water. We jumped into the truck again, tore down to the store, and bought six more Daredevils.

When we got back Joanne, having witnessed our luck with fishing, was roasting wieners for a hot-dog supper. "How much do those red-and-white things cost?" she wanted to know.

There was no time to answer. Greg and I ran onto the bridge for another shot at the salmon. We were working on our last Daredevil—the rest securely hooked onto underwater debris—when another logging truck pulled up. The driver took out his fishing pole.

"We're having terrible luck with snags," I told him.

"Yeah, well, you haf'ta put your lure over here," he said as he perfectly cast his Daredevil into the roiling water. In seconds he pulled up a large salmon, hooked by the belly with the lure.

"Holy smoke!" I gasped. "What great luck!"

"Not really," he said. "The salmon don't swallow the lure. They bump up against it to check it out and when they do you jerk the line and snag 'em."

Greg and I stared at each other, openmouthed. It was then I realized that fishing wasn't just dumb luck. It required skills I'd never had. That was my last fishing trip.

Until the other day.

My friend Jeff was telling me about the nice brook trout he'd caught the day before, and it aroused ancient memories of my angling adventures.

"Let's go fishing," I said.

"When's the last time you went fishing?" he asked.

"Uh . . . thirty-five years ago."

Jeff rolled his eyes. "Well, go get a license and a pole."

I picked up a fishing license at Dunhams and then cruised over to Wal-Mart where I found just what I needed—a nifty, four-foot fluorescent-green rod. It came complete with a plastic spinning reel pre-spooled with line, which was a big selling point because I didn't have the foggiest memory of how to mount line in a reel. The whole rig cost $13.50—much more than I'd ever paid as a kid—but what the heck, money was no object. I wanted the very best.

We headed out to Lake Michigamme. Our friend Lidia came along, too, which was a good thing because I wound up borrowing hooks, bobbers, and worms from her tackle box. Jeff reminded me that I first had to put a leader on the line and then even tied it on for me since I couldn't remember if it required a special knot.

Jeff lent me one of his spoon lures, and just like thirty-five years before, I promptly snagged it on something in the water. Fortunately, it came loose, dragging a huge clump of lake weed from the lake bottom.

"Reel it in faster so it doesn't snag on the bottom," Jeff told me.

I cast the lure out again and then began reeling it in like crazy. But the lure, sensing who was at the other end of the line, dove to the bottom and grabbed onto another hefty mass of weeds to bring back to me.

I finally decided to switch over to worms and a bobber. I had an awful time trying to get the worm on the hook until it dawned on me that the last time I baited a hook my eyesight was a lot better. I put my glasses on, and that did the trick.

I cast the worm out and let it sit for several minutes, keeping an eye on the bobber. When I reeled it in to see if the worm was still on the hook, I immediately snagged it on a lily pad sitting on the water. I gave the line a vicious yank. The line snapped, leaving the hook, leader, sinker, and bobber out in the lily pads.

"Whaddaya say we head to Ishpeming for lunch?" I asked Jeff and Lidia.

"Okay," Lidia said. "But first take those worm entrails off your eyeglasses."

We packed up. Jeff stated that the fishing wasn't good anyway with the stiff east wind blowing off the water. He'd caught one bass but released it because he preferred trout. Lidia'd had one on her line, but it got away. Nonetheless, if we'd compared weight of catch, I would've been the hands-down winner with the fifty pounds of assorted vegetation that I reeled in. I'm just glad I didn't have to eat what I caught.

ഇൻരു

A SHORT TRIP TO CANADA

This summer I've been fairly successful in expanding the network of establishments that sells my books. I've burned up a lot of gas ferreting out bookstores and gift shops in Michigan and Wisconsin. The effort has paid off so well that I began thinking, why not go international? Why not Canada? I loaded up the trunk of my new Buick with books and set out for Thunder Bay, Ontario.

A friend of mine went along. Lidia has helped me out on many a book-selling trip around Michigan this summer. Somehow she has the uncanny ability to point out shops and even restaurants and gas stations that wind up ordering my books. So we headed up the western shore of Lake Superior toward the Canadian border. I sold books at several stores in Minnesota, so it appeared that it would be a profitable trip.

While we were waiting in the long line at the Canadian border we set our wristwatches and the car clock one hour ahead since we were crossing back into the Eastern time zone.

Finally, we made our way up to the window at the Canadian border station. A uniformed official asked the usual questions: where were we born, purpose of the visit, etc. Then he wanted to know if we were bringing anything into Canada.

"Yes," I said. "I'm an author/publisher, and I have books in the trunk of the car. I'm going to try to sell them to the bookstores and gift shops in Thunder Bay."

He filled out a form and handed it to me. "Park your car over here on the left and take this form inside to the Immigration desk."

I moved the car to the side of the building. "Now, don't fib to them," Lidia advised.

"Of course not! What can they do to me for telling the truth?"

"I'm waiting here in the car," Lidia said. "I don't want to watch this."

The man at the Immigration desk took the form and looked it over. "What's the retail price of your book?" he asked.

"I've written several different books, and the prices vary."

Apparently the form only had room for one number. "Give me an average price."

I came up with a number. He jotted it down and handed the form back to me. "Take this over to the next counter and someone will help you." I moved on to another uniformed person, a woman.

"I'll have to see your books," she said.

She followed me out to the Buick. Lidia stuck her head out the car window and watched us nervously as I opened the trunk. The official looked over the several cases of books. "How many books are there?"

"I really don't know," I admitted.

"We'll have to count them," she said.

"It'll go a lot faster if you help me count," I said, wanting to get a little revenge on the Canadian government.

In the hot sun we pulled box after box out of the trunk and emptied each one to get an exact book count. After some time we arrived at a number and then filled up the boxes again and loaded them back into the trunk.

I followed her back into the building. "What now?" I asked her.

"You'll have to pay duty on the books before you can bring them into Canada."

"Duty?" I could feel my blood pressure rising. "How much duty?"

The woman punched numbers into her computer for several seconds and gave me the U.S. dollar figure for the duty. It came to about $1.50 per book, which would put a sizable dent in my profit margin.

"I don't know if I'll even sell *ANY* of the books in Canada. It's a speculative trip. I could wind up bringing them all back into the U.S."

She smiled. "Well, don't worry. In that event the Canadian government will be happy to reimburse you for the duty on any unsold books. All you have to do is apply for the reimbursement when you return to the border."

I could see it now. Unloading all of the books from the trunk of the car again, taking them out of the boxes, and recounting them. Then filling out a ton of paperwork to send in to Ottawa and maybe, just maybe, getting some money back after a six-month wait.

"Where do I turn to get back into the United States?" I asked.

Grumbling, I got back into the car. "Set the car clock back an hour," I told Lidia. "We're heading back into Minnesota."

"You lied to them, didn't you?" Lidia said.

"No, I didn't lie. That was the problem."

We had been in Canada for all of forty minutes. Lidia fiddled with the clock as we headed back across the border. "I don't know if my body can stand this time-zone whiplash," she said.

So my effort to go international fizzled. If I'd known about the duty, it would have been tempting to keep my mouth shut about the books. On the other hand, if I'd done that, it would have really gotten interesting if the Canadians had decided to look in the trunk of my car.

<u>1st Canadian border official:</u> "Books? This old goat is smuggling books into Canada? Dig around in the bottom of those boxes. He's got to have something in there besides books."

<u>2nd Canadian border official:</u> "Nope. Nothing but books."

<u>1st Canadian:</u> "Rip out a page from one of them and send it over to the lab in Winnipeg. It's probably impregnated with cocaine or something. Better yet, send the whole book. Tell them to analyze the binding glue. It might be plastic explosive."

<u>2nd Canadian:</u> "Maybe the books are just pornographic material."

<u>1st Canadian:</u> "Hmm . . . it's possible. While you're booking the driver I'll sit down and read."

₭₡

ADVENTURES WITH A STAY-AT-HOME DAD

Sixty years ago, long before the phrase was invented, my father was a stay-at-home dad. I was the other party involved. During the depression the old man was a struggling farmer, growing potatoes on a plot of land in West Ishpeming next to US-41 where Snyder Drug is now. *Growing* the potatoes wasn't the struggle; *selling* them was. It reached the point where he had to trade potatoes at the local stores for groceries and other essentials.

In 1940 my father finally had to give up farming. Then in 1941 things began looking up. My mother landed a good-paying job as a seamstress at the Gossard Company in Ishpeming. There was one problem. Because I was only eight years old, someone needed to stay home to see that I got dressed in the morning, make me breakfast, be sure that I got off to school on time, and generally keep house. My sister Esther—ten years older—had already gone off to college, so guess who got stuck with the job.

I remember the first morning that my father was in charge of the household. I came downstairs and sat at the kitchen table.

"Whaddaya want for breakfast?" the old man asked.

"Pancakes!" I shouted. This was going to be great. I loved pancakes, but my mother only made them on special occasions. And she never ever *asked* me what I wanted for breakfast; I always got fed hot nourishing oatmeal during the school year, whether I liked it or not.

The old man rooted around among the pots and pans in the pantry and came up with the biggest frying pan he could find. He threw a couple of hefty logs into the kitchen stove and put the frying pan on top to heat while he tried to figure out how to make the batter. After reading the instructions on the Aunt Jemima box he poured the ingredients into a big bowl and stirred it up. The resulting sludge didn't exactly resemble my mother's pancake batter, and we both knew it. There was a powdery scum on the surface with large lumps floating here and there. The old man finally decided that it would be simpler to make just one pancake, so he poured all the batter into the hot frying pan.

The pancake came out very large—about the size of a manhole cover—and thick. It was black and hard on the bottom and sort of white and pasty on top. Syrup just puddled on it like an oil slick. It didn't taste very good, but the old man kept watching to see if I liked it, so I ate the whole thing.

That evening my mother asked me what I'd had for breakfast.

"A pancake," I said.

Knowing how much I loved pancakes, she got suspicious. "Only one?"

"One was enough."

The next day when I came home for lunch my father had already heated up some Campbell's chicken noodle soup.

"Ya want anything else?" he asked.

"Can I have some toast to go with the soup?"

The old man tossed two slices of bread on top of the wood stove. When the bread started to smoke he turned them over and did the other side. The burnt toast looked terrible, but with butter and jam it wasn't half bad.

I was never very particular about what I wore to school, and the old man didn't see any reason to worry about it either. One day the third-grade teacher looked at my mismatched socks and asked me who had dressed me that morning.

"I dress myself," I said with pride. However, not wanting to take the full credit, I added, "My father helps me a little bit, though."

The teacher nodded and then asked me where my mother was.

One day my father decided that I should help him keep the house straightened up. He showed me how simple it was.

"Ya put everything outta sight," he said. To demonstrate his point he picked up yesterday's *Mining Journal* off the carpet and jammed it into a drawer in our living-room library table. That didn't look too hard, so I went around the house and did the same thing. The house then looked pretty good to the old man and me.

Weeks later when my mother was finding odd things in odd places: a toy fire truck in with my clean underwear, a dirty coffee cup in the refrigerator vegetable bin, a dog bone in a kitchen drawer, she realized that having my father in charge of the home front wasn't going to work out.

Mom managed to get her Gossard schedule adjusted so she could be at home to inspect my clothes, make my breakfast, and see me off to school. Things drifted back to normal, and I didn't see pancakes for breakfast for a long time.

Even now, though, sixty years later, I find myself thinking that a couple of pieces of burnt toast for breakfast would really taste good.

ৰ০৫৪

1940'S COMFORT FOOD

I was in Econo Foods the other day and happened to spot Trenary Toast. Hard to believe, but it's been seven years since I moved back to the U.P., and I've never had Trenary Toast. It looked like the rusk toast I remember as a kid, so I bought a package, took it home, and dunked a slice in my coffee. It *was* the same and soooo good. It made me feel like I was ten years old.

I was introduced to rusk (a.k.a. Trenary) toast when I was first allowed to drink coffee. My father showed me how to dunk it in coffee, long enough to soggy it up properly but not so long that it broke off in the cup. Finn men dunked rusk toast in their breakfast coffee because they didn't have to put their false teeth in to chew it. For me it was a rite of passage into manhood.

The Trenary Toast made me think of other food I enjoyed as a kid. I loved cold breakfast cereal. During the 1940's there were only a handful of cold cereals—corn flakes, Cheerios, Wheaties, Kix, and Grape Nuts are what I remember. As far as my mother was concerned, Quaker's oatmeal was the only cereal fit to eat, and she wanted to feed it to me every morning. But Quaker's oatmeal didn't have box tops, so I lobbied hard for Wheaties for enough box tops to get things like Jack Armstrong's Egyptian Whistle Ring to ward off wrongdoers or the neat World War II cardboard fighter-plane models.

I must have grown six inches on Wheaties acquiring all the prizes that Jack Armstrong hawked.

As a kid I never liked vegetables, and I certainly didn't have much use for the boiled potatoes that my mother served, but do-it-yourself roasted potatoes were another story. My friend Jeff and I would pile up chunks of cardboard, sticks, and old boards in the middle of the alley and build a fire. We'd impale raw potatoes—unwashed, of course—on sticks and roast them over the fire. You knew the potatoes were done when there was a half inch of jet-black carbon on the skin, and the stick they were on burned through and the potatoes fell into the fire. We fished them out and ate them. The part of the stick inside the potato provided a lot of good fiber, and the layer of roasted dirt gave it a tangy, musty flavor. Mmmm, mmmm, good.

Speaking of vegetables, right after the war started, my mother told me we were going to plant a victory garden, and that I could be the chief gardener. At age nine I thought that vegetables were born at the A & P, but she explained the facts of life (about plants, that is) and how you tucked seeds into the ground and watered them, and they popped up and grew into healthy vegetables. I got very enthusiastic and ran down to Leffler's store in Ishpeming and picked out seeds. After hoeing up a patch of ground in our backyard, I planted carrot, lettuce, and radish seeds. During the summer of '42 I watered the garden religiously. Sure enough, green sprouts appeared like magic and leafed out. I was bursting with pride. Then one day my mother told me to harvest the victory-garden vegetables. I ran out and pulled up carrots, radishes, and lettuce leaves, thoroughly excited that I'd actually grown this stuff all by myself.

That night a large salad bowl sat on the supper table. My mother gave me a generous helping of salad, and without thinking I dug in. After a few chews I realized that I was eating the vegetables that I grew. I hated vegetables. I thought we were going to ship those victory-garden vegetables to the GI's overseas. I didn't know I had to eat the stuff myself. After that I lost a lot of enthusiasm for victory gardens.

We had chokecherry trees in our yard. During the summer Jeff and I would wait until the birds started to eat the chokecherries (the birds knew when they were ripe), and then we'd climb the trees and gorge ourselves. Chokecherry juice is astringent enough to take the paint right off your car, but in those days we had cast-iron stomachs.

I used to get a nickel for candy on Saturday for the Ishpeming Theater matinee, but during the rest of the week candy was in short supply. One candy substitute was raw rhubarb. That's right, raw rhubarb. Rhubarb—we called it pie plant—grew wild in our back yard, and I'd cut off a stalk, dip one end in sugar, and bite off a hunk. It goes without saying that this was definitely an acquired taste.

I remember graham-cracker mush. I'd put graham crackers in a bowl and pour milk over them. When they got soggy I'd mush them up with a spoon and eat them. This was even better than cold cereal, but the Nabisco graham-cracker box didn't offer any box-top prizes, so the mush ranked a distant second in breakfast priorities.

Another kid treat I really enjoyed was catsup sandwiches. I used to go across the railroad tracks to Jeff's house where his mother made them for us. A true catsup sandwich had to be made with store-bought white bread where the pasty dough would soak up the catsup to make a nice gooey reddish mess. It was delicious, although Jeff now claims that he got good and sick of catsup and hasn't touched the stuff since 1945.

಴ಀಃ

MEMORIES OF HIDEOUTS

When I was little all boys had hideouts. We originally got the idea from the crooks in the Saturday-matinee westerns. They lived in hideouts where they plotted against Tom Mix, Gene Autry, and the other white-hatted heroes. We hated the bad guys and threw empty Cracker Jack boxes at them whenever they appeared on the screen, but we loved their hideouts and built our own.

My very first hideout was, believe it or not, in our living room. We had a large wood-burning parlor stove in one corner but far enough away from the walls so the wallpaper wouldn't catch fire. Between the stove and the corner was a little space that, at age five, only I could crawl into. I wanted to hide from my mother, and she wouldn't fit in the space. I proudly hung all of my kindergarten artwork on the walls in the hideout and also kept other valuable possessions in there—tinkertoy projects, crayons, favorite marbles, and a prized assortment of cast-iron toy cars. During the winter, with the stove going full blast, it got hotter than the hinges of Hades back there, and wearing my long underwear, I got pretty ripe. But I endured it because, after all, this was my hideout.

Also in the winter my friend Jeff and I built hideouts in the snow. High snowbanks were plentiful, and using shovels we'd tunnel into one and hollow out the inside to make our hideout. We would bring in sandwiches and soda pop and then have to gulp down the snacks before they froze.

One real downside of snow hideouts were the cave-ins. More often than not the roof of the hideout would collapse in on us, and we'd have to claw our way out, gasping for air.

At age eight I realized that a bigger, more substantial hideout was needed. That summer Jeff and I embarked on building one in my backyard, with wooden walls and a roof, no less. My father, with his wagon and team of horses, had a job hauling garbage from the A&P, and he'd bring home wagon-loads of empty wooden crates to be used for firewood. So Jeff and I had plenty of building material. We grabbed hammers and set about disassembling the old crates, painstakingly pulling out the nails and pounding them straight for future use. (I thought everyone did that. I was a teenager before I realized that hardware stores sold new nails.)

When my father found us in the backyard, pulling the crates apart, he asked us what we were doing. I told him about the hideout plan. The old man thought that every Finn should have some carpentry skills, so he went along with the idea. In fact, to get us started, he cut up some two-by-fours and did the framing. To keep it simple he nailed one end of the frame to the outside wall of our house and the opposite end to a nearby section of the backyard fence. He then turned the tools over to Jeff and me and told us we were now on our own.

Jeff and I attacked the job vigorously, smashing our fingers with the large hammers as we nailed apple-, celery-, and fish-crate boards to the hideout frame to form the walls and roof. It was perfectly engineered with windows in the front and rear walls for returning fire at any gang of Catholic kids that might invade the backyard.

We completed the job in a single day. Just as we were pounding in the final nails, my mother came out the back door to see what the racket was all about. She had a job at the Gossard factory and was at work when we had started the project that morning.

She was amazed to find that we had added a new wing on the house. "What in the world is that?"

I told her that it was our new hideout. She said that it was the ugliest thing she'd ever seen and told us to tear it down.

"But Pop helped us build it."

"Your father had a hand in *THIS*?"

"Yup."

She shook her head and went back into the house. At the supper table the old man convinced her that the hideout couldn't be seen from the street, so there was no harm in leaving it there.

The hideout had one problem. When Jeff and I nailed on the roof boards we neglected to go inside and bend the nail points back into the wood. We had an inverted bed of spikes in the ceiling.

My mother stared at me during supper. "You've got all kinds of blood on the top of your head."

"Yeah, well . . . the hideout ceiling is too low."

She sighed. "I'll sure be glad when school starts."

The hideout needed one more thing. A lookout post. Jeff and I nailed a wooden bushel basket to a limb high up in a tree in the backyard. That way we could spot the Catholic kids coming down the alley and then climb down to make adequate preparations.

One day Jeff and I had crammed ourselves into the lookout basket when my mother spotted us up in the tree.

"You two come down this minute!"

"It's okay, Mom. We got it nailed real good to the tree." The basket swayed precariously in the breeze.

"Get down here right now! School starts on Monday, and we're going down to Penny's and get you some new clothes."

So my hideout days were over. By the next summer the hideout had lost its appeal because there were other things like baseball to do.

I still have fond memories of hideouts, though, as I'm sure many of you do.

Of course, there are many Yoopers who still have their hideouts, except now they call them camps, and they're hiding out from wives, not mothers.

ഇ✆ഌ

DO YOU REMEMBER WHEN?

I get a lot of e-mail from old geez . . . , I mean senior citizens on the subject of reminiscing, but this one I received recently from a friend in California tops the list. I've added a few of my own ideas as well.

Do you remember when . . .

No one ever lost their car keys because they were always in the ignition?

Schools threatened to keep a kid back a grade if he failed . . . and they did?

You pulled into a service station and actually got service—oil checked, windshield cleaned, pressure checked on all four tires, and the air was *FREE?* And you got trading stamps to boot?

Kids played baseball with no adults around to help with the rules of the game?

Women wore nylons that came in two pieces?

You'd reach into a muddy gutter for a penny?

It took five minutes for your black-and-white TV set to warm up?

Nobody owned a purebred dog?

Being sent to the principal's office was nothing compared to the fate awaiting you at home?

Telephone numbers had a word prefix, and you had to talk to a real live operator to call long distance?

Catching fireflies could happily occupy an entire summer evening?

Parents swatted unruly children and didn't get sued?

Having a weapon in school meant being caught with a slingshot?

The worst thing you could catch from the opposite sex was "cooties?"

Families sat around in the evening and listened to the radio?

Baseball cards in the spokes transformed any bike into a motorcycle?

Water balloons were the ultimate weapon?

Taking drugs meant swallowing aspirin?

Spinning around, getting dizzy, and falling down was cause for giggles?

Laundry detergent had free glasses, dishes, or towels hidden inside the box?

There were only two types of sneakers, one for girls and one for boys, and the only time you wore them at school was in gym class?

Having the postman deliver a package from Sears Roebuck was enough excitement for one day?

The worst thing you could do in school was flunk a test or chew gum?

Baseball players began making so much money that people said it wouldn't be long before they'd be making more than the President of the United States?

Electric typewriters were a technological breakthrough?

People were afraid that Volkswagens would open the door to foreign imports?

The good guys always won and crime didn't pay?

Everyone was shocked when Clark Gable said "damn" in *Gone*

With the Wind?

It was outrageous when the post office began charging seven cents just to mail a letter?

You had to add, subtract, multiply and divide by hand?

Erasers had to be clapped outside the school door?

Kids earned a quarter-a-week allowance by hauling ashes from the kitchen stove?

You had to skim the cream off the top of the milk bottle?

The only solar power was drying the wash on the clothes line?

Doctors made house calls?

Going downtown was a big deal?

A one-car garage was considered a luxury?

There was always a barrel of pickles sitting in the corner grocery store?

Your telephone rang and the caller was someone you knew who wasn't trying to sell you a new long-distance carrier?

Nearly everyone's mom was at home when the kids got home from school?

Stuff from the drug store came without safety caps and hermetic seals because no one had yet tried to poison a perfect stranger?

You might want to pass these on to anyone afflicted with high blood pressure, acid reflux, or heart palpitations to give them a bit of relief from their "sophisticated" life.

∞∞

DECISIONS UNDER FIRE

For many years I lived in Southern California, so when the recent wildfires were burning I was glued to the TV set. My heart went out to the people whose homes were in the path of the fires.

You see, it also happened to me.

Can there ever be a lighter side to an ordeal like that? You be the judge.

In 1970 my wife, Joanne, and I were the proud owners of first and second mortgages on a beautiful hillside home in Topanga Canyon, California. One Friday in September a wildfire broke out in Malibu Canyon, about fifteen miles from our Topanga place. That night we watched the fire on TV, but, what the heck, we weren't concerned. After all, it was fifteen miles away.

The next morning Joanne, who was into showing dogs at the time, drove to Lawndale, an LA suburb, to participate in a show. I went off in my pickup truck to do the weekly grocery shopping in nearby Woodland Hills. As I drove out of Topanga Canyon, I could see smoke from the Malibu fire, a long way off in the distance.

An hour later I was heading home. Just around a curve at the mouth of the canyon I saw the blazing Malibu fire, but now it was less than a mile away, moving rapidly toward Topanga Canyon.

The California Highway Patrol had already set up a roadblock on the narrow two-lane road going into Topanga Canyon. I stopped and flashed my driver's license to an officer to show him that I was a canyon resident.

"The canyon's under a mandatory evacuation order," he snapped. "You've got thirty minutes to get out. Take only your valuables."

Tromping on the gas pedal, I careened around the curves on the canyon road and pulled into our driveway. My fifteen-year-old stepson, Greg, was standing by the garage.

"There's cops driving up and down the road," he said. "They're telling us to get out."

"I know. We've got about fifteen minutes to load up our valuables and leave."

Greg gave me a vacant teenage stare. "Valuables?"

"Yes. Take only the things you value the most."

We both ran into the house and began gathering possessions. Joanne and I played guitar, so I grabbed the guitars and put them in the bed of the pickup. Greg lugged out a pair of large speakers, a turntable, and his 200-watt amplifier. Next he brought out his record collection.

Records! I had many Peter, Paul, and Mary LP's, so I hustled into the house and got them. I also picked up my single-shot .22 rifle. Oh, boy, I almost forgot my golf clubs. I ran to the hall closet and got them. And my priceless folk-song-book collection! I threw them in two grocery bags and brought them out to the truck.

A highway patrol drove by with a bullhorn. "THIS IS A MANDATORY FIRE EVACUATION. YOU HAVE FIVE MINUTES TO LEAVE."

Greg, now realizing that this was a bona fide emergency, ran to the kitchen and grabbed his box of Ding Dongs. Figuring that we may be in for some hectic days ahead, I took a gallon jug of wine from the refrigerator.

We jumped in the loaded pickup and sped down the canyon road. By now the sky was a deep shade of gray from the smoke.

"Did Mom take Thunderball with her?" Greg asked. We had three dogs, two purebred Welsh corgis and Thunderball, a mixed breed.

"She's at a breed show," I said. "Maybe she left him at home." I turned the truck around and went back to the house.

Thunderball was asleep under a living-room chair.

I rousted him and we took off again. A half hour later we arrived at the Lawndale dog show, and I told Joanne what had happened.

She stared at the loaded pickup. "I hope you remembered our birth certificates."

"Uh . . . well . . . no."

"How about my prescription?"

"Prescription? What prescription?"

Her eyes narrowed, and she leaned over close to me. "My birth-control pills, you idiot."

"Uh-oh."

"If you're thinking of resuming our love life anytime soon you'd better pray that the house doesn't burn down. How about the home-owners insurance policy?"

"I didn't take it, but the insurance company has a copy of it."

"You handled all of that. Who's the insurance company?"

"Uh . . . I don't remember. I'm sure it'll come to me."

Where did you park the trailer?" she asked.

"Ohmigawd!" I had forgotten the trailer. We had just bought a twenty-foot travel trailer to use on summer vacations. I was storing it in an empty lot across the road from our house.

Joanne's mouth hung open. "You left our brand-new trailer, which we just began making monthly payments on, in the path of a wildfire?"

"I'm going back," I said.

"While you're there, bring me some clean underwear," Joanne said.

I drove up to Topanga Canyon and stopped at the roadblock.

"Didn't you come through here a couple of times already this morning?" the highway-patrol officer said.

"I forgot my trailer, and my wife told me to get her some clean underwear."

The officer rolled his eyes. "They're making aerial water drops on the fire now, which is the only reason I'll let you in. Get the *!!@#%! trailer and your wife's underwear and get back out here!"

It was a close call, but that day the firefighters stopped the blaze about three hundred yards from our house. Four days later we were back home.

For all you guys who live close to the woods, my advice is this: think ahead. Make a list of all of your essential valuables, and then put them in a box. Keep the box by the door in the event you have to run from a forest fire.

Come to think of it, let your wife handle this. Women seem to be better at that sort of thing.

෩෨

THANKSGIVING WITH ALL THE STUFFING

I know it's a time-honored tradition to eat yourself silly on Thanksgiving, but I don't do that anymore. I practice restraint now.

It's all because of one fateful turkey day, a long time ago.

In 1952 I had completed my freshman year at the University of Michigan. That summer I took a six-month co-op job as an engineer trainee at White Sands Proving Ground (now White Sands Missile Range) in New Mexico.

As summer faded into late fall, the New Mexico weather began resembling our Michigan weather—cold, gray, and generally ugly. November was the beginning of the sandstorm season. Outdoors you had to shield your eyes from the blowing sand and simultaneously dodge the tumbleweeds rocketing across the desert floor in the high winds.

This would be the first Thanksgiving that I wasn't at home, and I was especially homesick. I would miss my mother's succulent roast turkey, hot buttered sweet potatoes, cranberry sauce, homemade dressing, and the rest of the goodies. To make matters worse, I hadn't even been invited out for Thanksgiving dinner. There were six of us U of M co-op engineering students, and we all lived in a small Quonset hut on the White Sands army base. Four of the U of M guys had been invited to share Thanksgiving dinner with fellow workers who lived in nearby towns. But Bob Kovacs and I were left at the Quonset hut.

It was going to be a grim, depressing day. Bob and I lay on our bunk beds, listening to the angry sand clawing at the metal walls of the Quonset.

"You want to try the Thanksgiving dinner over at the NCO club?" Bob asked.

"How much is it?"

"Fifty cents."

"Fifty cents?" I cried. "You wanna pay that much for *ONE* dinner?" We took our meals at the Enlisted Men's Mess where five cents got us a breakfast of K ration powdered scrambled eggs left over from World War II (That's no lie.). Lunch and dinner cost a dime each, but the quality wasn't any better. To spend fifty cents on a meal prepared by the U.S. Army was sheer folly.

"Some of the guys I know say it's supposed to be pretty good," Bob said. "Let's give it a try."

Bob and I put on our coats and went out, leaning into the fierce sandy wind as we headed for the Noncommissioned Officers' (NCO) Club. We handed our fifty cents to a corporal at the door and looked around in utter amazement. Normally, the NCO Club resembled a sleazy juke joint where sergeants and corporals ate gray, greasy hamburgers washed down with beer out of the can while listening to Ernest Tubbs on the Wurlitzer.

Today it was very different. There were white tablecloths on the chipped formica tables. Orange and brown crepe streamers hung from the ceiling. GI's in white starched aprons stood behind the counter, waiting to serve us.

Bob sniffed the air. "That smells like *REAL* food."

A smiling GI standing by a huge, golden-brown turkey handed me a real plate, not the tin tray we were used to eating from.

"Would you like white or dark meat, sir?"

No one on the base had ever called me "sir."

Bob and I were handed heaping plates, and we found a table and dug in with gusto. We scarfed down thick slices of turkey, mounds of mashed potatoes swimming in gravy, dressing, cranberry sauce, yams, and assorted vegetables. And then we went back for another helping. After that we each put away two slices of pie—one pumpkin and one mincemeat. It was all delicious.

We slowly waddled back to the Quonset. The sandstorm didn't bother us one bit now because we were both carrying a lot of ballast.

The two of us were sprawled on our backs in our bunks, burping contentedly and thinking how we wouldn't need to eat the putrid mess-hall food until at least Tuesday when the hall phone rang. I struggled to my feet and dragged my stomach over to the phone.

"This is Paul." Paul Szyperski, another U of M co-oper, had gone to Las Cruces for Thanksgiving with Ramon Martinez, a fellow worker. "Hey, have I got a surprise for you two."

I stifled a mince-meat-flavored belch. "What's that, Paul?"

"Grab the three o'clock bus to Las Cruces. I've wrangled a Thanksgiving dinner at the Martinez's for you and Kovacs."

I laughed hysterically and told Paul about our huge dinner at the NCO Club, and that there was no way we could come into Las Cruces and eat another one.

Paul got very testy. "You gotta come! I told Ramon and his wife how you guys were spending the day all alone in the Quonset. Ramon went to the store and bought another turkey to be able to feed all of us. His wife has it in the oven right now."

Thirty minutes later Kovacs and I were on the bus to Las Cruces, a town twenty-eight miles from the proving ground.

"I can't believe we're doing this," I said.

"Maybe we should open the bus window and throw up, "Bob

126

suggested. "That's what the Romans used to do between feasts"

Paul Szyperski and Ramon Martinez met us at the bus stop in downtown Las Cruces and took us to the Martinez home. As we got out of the car, Paul whispered to me, "Whatever you do, don't tell Ramon's wife that you two have already had a big dinner."

Mrs. Martinez, a jolly, roly-poly woman was standing at the front door. "You're just in time. The food is on the table. Ramon, look how skinny these two boys are! I'm going to have to do something about that!" She led us into the dining room. Bob and I carefully lowered our bloated bodies into chairs at the table loaded with steaming dishes.

I had it in mind to take teeny, tiny portions, but at the head of the table Ramon did the honors. He dished out the servings and passed them down. On my plate was a turkey drumstick the size of a rhinoceros haunch, flanked by gigantic mounds of mashed potatoes, dressing and vegetables.

"Okay, you men," Mrs. Martinez chirped cheerfully. "I want to see those plates cleaned."

I slowly and methodically began putting food into my mouth. Within fifteen minutes the chow was backing up in my esophagus, and I had to swallow repeatedly to keep it down. Miraculously, I got the plate nearly empty. My stomach was screaming in protest, bringing tears to my eyes.

Mrs. Martinez noticed this. "You're crying. What's wrong?"

"Nothing, ma'am. It's tears of happiness for all your kindness."

That was the wrong thing to say. Smiling broadly, Ramon's wife whisked my plate away and promptly filled it up again.

I don't remember much about the rest of the meal except that toward the end I began hallucinating. When dessert was served, the scoop of vanilla ice cream on top of my pumpkin pie ala mode sprouted arms and legs, sprang off the pie to my throat, and began choking me. When the meal was finally over, Kovacs, his face now grayish green, sat there with head bowed and eyes shut. He was thanking the good Lord for survival.

Seriously, I wish you all a very happy Thanksgiving and hope that you'll have plenty of turkey to go around. I personally will have my usual toasted cheese sandwich and an apple.

ഇറ

CHRISTMASES IN ISHPEMING

I don't remember a thing about my first Christmas in Ishpeming since I was only eight months old, and my major priorities were napping and sucking up food.

The second Christmas was pretty vague, too, but my mother later told me that by then I was more mobile, and I literally kicked off the season with a bang. She had placed me on the rug in the front room (what we called the living room back then) near the decorated Christmas tree so that I could enjoy the colored lights. I must have thought the lights were pretty neat because I reached for one, giving a spruce branch a sharp yank. The whole tree toppled over on top of me, boinking ornaments off my head.

My first clear recollection of Christmas was when I was four. It was my rookie year in Sunday School at the Ishpeming Bethel Lutheran Church, and we were putting on a gala Christmas Eve program for the congregation. I was part of the grand finale. Somehow I had managed to memorize the Twenty-Third Psalm, and I was to stand up in front of God and everybody and recite it. For weeks I'd practiced at home and got so good that I could rattle it off in my sleep. The big night arrived. Standing and facing the congregation that evening, I was cruising along just fine, the words flowing effortlessly from my mouth.

That is, until I locked eyes with my teenaged sister.

Esther was sitting in the fourth row, and began giving me her Harpo Marx impression—bulging crossed eyes and a wide, slack-jaw grin. She knew it would mess me up, and that's exactly what happened. Three lines from the end I ground to a halt. I stumbled to my seat amid sympathetic smiles from the congregation. After the program I went up to my mother and ratted on Esther, but my conniving sister disclaimed all knowledge of the deed and was never prosecuted.

A few weeks before Christmas the city of Ishpeming would put up a large Christmas tree on a little plot of land next to the Mather Inn. Every year there was one night when Santa would sit next to the lighted tree and pass out popcorn balls to the kids. Santa's "Merry Christmas! HO! HO! HO!" was always very enthusiastic, mainly, I think, because to keep out the cold he was sipping on a beverage he had in a brown paper bag. Even as a kid I never liked popcorn, but I was always there, shivering in the long line, waiting to get my popcorn ball. What the heck, the popcorn was free and it was Christmas.

Of course we drew names at school to exchange presents on the day before Christmas vacation. I remember in the fourth grade I drew the name of the girl who sat in front of me—a real looker with long graceful legs. It drove me crazy trying to think of something keen to buy this gorgeous beauty. My mother convinced me that a model Japanese Zero fighter plane wasn't such a good idea, so I settled for a barrette. I often wonder what happened to that girl. I'm not going to try to look her up, though. She may have lost her looks by now.

I always hung up a stocking on Christmas Eve. And I quickly wised up to the fact that my father had a much larger foot, so I would hang one of his big woolen hunting socks to get more goodies. We didn't have a fireplace so the sock got hung by taping it to the edge of the library table. The "stocking stuffer" presents in those days were mostly edibles. Santa usually put oranges and nuts in my sock.

Kids nowadays would be pretty put out to find stuff like that in their Christmas stocking, but I didn't mind at all because the only time I saw oranges and nuts was at Christmas.

Like all kids, I tried to wait up for Santa Claus and catch him in the act of putting presents under the tree. I had devised a clever plan for doing this. My upstairs bedroom had a floor register that allowed the heat to drift up from downstairs. When it was open the register also served as an excellent spying device. I could look through it and watch and hear what was going on in the front room. On Christmas Eve I would lie on the bedroom floor next to the register and wait for Santa. My parents, of course, knew this, so they'd wait till I'd fallen asleep on the floor and then come up and put me to bed.

But at four o'clock on Christmas morning I was wide awake. I'd dash downstairs in my button-up sleeping suit to try to catch Santa Claus. But the sneaky devil had already been there, stuffing my old man's sock taped to the library table with oranges and nuts and putting presents under the tree. I was the only one up at that hour, and the fires in the kitchen and front-room stoves had long since gone out. It was bone-chilling cold in the house, but it didn't bother me in the least. It was Christmas morning, and there were presents to open.

My mother and I always left a big array of snacks on the kitchen table for Santa—sweet rolls, date-delight cakes, and gingerbread cookies. All that was left early Christmas morning were a few crumbs. After eating all of that food, I figured that Santa Claus surely must have gotten stuck in a few chimneys after he left our house.

I don't remember how old I was when I began getting suspicious about Santa Claus, but I know it was because of our stovepipes. The only way Santa could have gotten into our house from the roof was through the stovepipes, and I suddenly realized that this was impossible. One Christmas morning I confronted the old man about it. He got evasive and said that Santa had come in through the kitchen door. But there were no tracks in the snow outside of our door, so I knew that it was just a tall tale.

I hope that Santa gets down your chimney okay and brings you everything you desire.

ഔ

GOODBYE, MY FRIEND

It's taken me quite awhile to write this piece because every time I sat down to do it I broke down and wept. On December 10, 2003, my friend Lidia Menchaca was killed in a traffic accident on US-2. She was driving down to lower Michigan to deliver Christmas presents to her 93-year-old mother and two brothers.

You only find a few really good friends in a lifetime, and Lidia was one of mine. We met just four years ago, but we crammed a lot of adventures, good times, and laughs into that short period.

The very first thing I noticed about Lidia was that her eyes sparkled. I mean it, they actually sparkled. I think it was because she felt that each day was an opportunity to learn or do something new and exciting. When she retired from teaching it wasn't from life. Retiring wasn't on her agenda. You were old only if you acted old, and she was having none of that.

When I first met Lidia she was taking music lessons, but not like normal people. She was taking piano, violin, and flute lessons, all at the same time. The following year Lidia took it into her head to swim the perimeter of Farmers Lake, so she went into training. I thought it was all idle chatter until I watched her do laps at the Sawyer YMCA pool. She swam for an hour nonstop. In the summer of 2002

Lidia swam completely around Farmers Lake as I followed in a boat, cheering her on.

This last summer Lidia decided to take up riflery. Over lunches at Peggy Sue's Cafe she kept my friend Jeff and me updated on her progress. Again, I didn't pay much attention until the day she brought in one of her targets. Using a .22-caliber target rifle, she'd put five rounds tight in the bull's-eye that could have been covered with a quarter. In a matter of a few weeks the woman had turned into another Annie Oakley.

Lidia and I took trips. We got within spitting distance of polar bears migrating through the town of Churchill on Hudson Bay. In the Caribbean, Lidia decided to try her hand at snorkeling. She was briefed on the technique, and proceeded into the water and began petting stingrays. Not exactly my cup of tea.

Lidia also accompanied me on summer book-selling trips around Michigan, Wisconsin, and Minnesota. She had the uncanny knack for ferreting out new places to sell my books. She would point at some lonely gas station along the road, saying, "Try this place." I'd pull into the station, and sure enough, the manager would look over my books and put in an order.

In November, Lidia, Jeff, and I drove to Dearborn to take in the Century of Flight exhibit at the Henry Ford Museum. Following the museum tour we strolled through nearby Greenfield Village and came upon an old merry-go-round that was operational.

"Let's go for a ride!" Lidia exclaimed.

I hadn't been on a merry-go-round in over sixty years, but I thought, why not?

Jeff elected to stand by and be the official photographer as Lidia and I selected our painted horses and climbed on. The operator put the merry-go-round in gear and the music began playing. Lidia and I went round and round, laughing and waving at Jeff on each turn. I had forgotten how much fun a carousel ride could be. But that was

Lidia's way; she would never let you forget how to stay young.

That was the last trip that Lidia and I took together.

So, goodbye, my friend. I'll always miss you. I hope that someday we'll meet again. I know that it'll be a good place if you're there. And who knows, maybe we'll find another merry-go-round.

Photo by Jeff Jacobs

℘℘

Biography

Jerry Harju was born in Ishpeming, Michigan, in 1933. He received a degree in engineering from the University of Michigan in 1957 and an MS from the University of Southern California in 1985. After thirty years as a manager in the Southern California aerospace industry, Jerry began writing as a second career. *Northern Reflections, Northern D'Lights, Northern Passages*, and *Northern Memories* are collections of humorous short stories about growing up in the Upper Peninsula in the 1930's and 40's. *The Class of '57* humorously describes Jerry's six years of "higher education" at the University of Michigan. University life then—with its 1950's attitudes on world affairs, morality, and women's roles in society—was much different from today. *Cold Cash* is Jerry's first novel, a wacky tale about two amateurs who try to solve their cash-flow problems by pulling a bank heist and getting away on snowmobiles. Typical of Harju's work, the robbery doesn't go as planned and is further complicated by two strong-willed women. The book won a Midwest Independent Publishers Association Book Achievement Award. *Here's what I think...* and his latest, *Way Back When,* are collections of selected humorous and nostalgic essays appearing for the past several years in the Marquette newspaper, the *Mining Journal.*

In addition to writing books and newspaper and magazine columns and running a publishing company, Jerry travels all over the globe.